TALES FROM THE MARBLE MOUNTAIN

HUGH GARDNER

TALES FROM THE
MARBLE MOUNTAIN

Part I · Beyond the Marble Mountain
Part II · Back to the Marble Mountain

Illustrated by Kiddell-Monroe

MEREDITH PRESS / *New York*

To Veronica, Helen and Joanna

First published in the United States of America by Meredith Press in 1969

Library of Congress Catalog Card Number: 69-12145 Printed in Great Britain for Meredith Press

CONTENTS

Contents (cont'd)

PART I
Beyond the Marble Mountain

I

How Bear got lost and met Goat

WHEN Bear was little he lived with his father and mother in a great big cave high up near the top of the Marble Mountain. He was a wandering sort of Bear even in those days, and his mother was always frightened he would get lost. So she gave him a huge bell to carry with him wherever he went. When he was far from home and didn't know the way back, he used to ring the bell loudly, and then sit down and wait until his mother came to fetch him. If he was too far away for his mother to hear, or if the wind was in the wrong direction, the birds would fly up to the cave to tell her little Bear was lost again in the forest, and to lead her to where he was.

One hot summer day, when Bear was quite big and old, he wandered off into the forest, carrying his bell as usual. He went on and on and on through the trees down the side of the Marble Mountain, farther than he'd ever been before. By and by he came to a clearing; and in the clearing he saw a great big busy swarm of bees.

So Bear walked up to the Queen Bee, who was sitting very proudly at the door of her hive, with all her courtiers buzzing round her, and bowed very politely. He stooped and put his ear close to her so that she wouldn't have to shout and they talked for a little while about the sun and the moon and the stars. Then Bear tactfully led the conversation round to honey, and asked her if he could have some. So the Queen Bee clapped her

wings, and all her courtiers went buzzing round the flowers of the forest to fetch honey for him. They brought back oodles of honey; and at first Bear was rather worried because he hadn't got a jar to put it in. He ate all he could; but there was still a lot left over.

Then he had a very clever idea. He took his huge bell and turned it upside down and filled it up with honey to the brim. Then he said 'good-bye' and 'thank you' to the Queen Bee and all her court; and, holding his bell-ful of honey upright, he walked on into the forest.

The farther he walked, the hotter it got, and the more tired he felt. He tried walking with his eyes shut; but that wasn't any good, because he kept walking into trees and having to apologise. So at last he lay down on a bank by a little running stream and fell fast asleep. He slept on and on and on, and as he slept he murmured in his sleep a long, drowsy rigmarole in which the word ' honey ' appeared again and again.

The sun got lower and lower, and suddenly Bear woke up. He felt cold and rather frightened. So he picked up his bell and swung it wildly to and fro. But of course it made no noise at all, because it was full up with honey. Bear was full up with honey, too, and found he couldn't eat a paw-ful more. He hadn't got the heart to scoop the honey out of the bell on to the ground and waste it. So he decided to try to find a way home by himself; and walked on fast, humming to keep himself warm.

After a bit he came to a notice saying ' Bear to

the left '. So he turned left. And a little bit
farther on he came to another notice saying ' Bear
to the right '. So he turned right. And a little
farther on still he came to another notice saying
' Bear straight ahead '. So he walked on and on
and on, until suddenly he came to the end of the
trees, and stepped right out on to the edge of a
wide, open plain.

By this time the sun had set and the moon had
risen high up above the Marble Mountain,
casting a silvery light on the great trees of the
forest behind him and the broad white plain
stretching out ahead of him. And Bear sat down
with his head between his hands, and felt very,
very sad and lonely, and wondered what he
ought to do next.

❧

As Bear sat down at the edge of the Great Plain,
he heard a gentle, pittery-pattery, prancy sort of
noise coming through the leaves of the forest
behind him. He turned round, and saw a
solemn, four-legged, white creature with great
curly horns and a long white beard trotting up to
him.

' I'm Goat,' said the creature, coming straight
to the point. ' I've just come down from the
mountain, and I'm going across the plains at

sunrise to-morrow morning to seek my fortune. Who are you?'

Bear got up and bowed very politely, and said, ' I'm Little Bear, and I'm lost and very cold.'

' Little Bear, indeed!' said Goat. ' A great hulking creature like you! Little, indeed! And how dare a creature like you, with all that gorgeous warm brown fur on you, talk about being cold to a creature like me, who has only got a long, white, straggly beard to wrap herself up in when its cold at nights!'

Bear was rather frightened of this disagreeable animal at first; but they went on talking; and after a bit Goat began to get a little more friendly. When she learnt that Bear was very thirsty, she

gave him some of her milk to drink; and Bear began to feel that he wasn't really lost any more now that Goat had found him.

After a bit, Goat said, ' It's much too late for you to think of going home to-night. You'll have to sleep in the sand with me. Then in the morning you can eat your honey for breakfast; and then you'll be able to ring your bell again, and your mother will come out from the cave and fetch you home.'

Now Bear had lived all his life on the mountain, where there was nothing but rocks and trees, and had never heard of sand; so he asked Goat what it was.

' That is sand,' said Goat, pointing with her hoof across the plain. ' All of it is sand for miles and miles and miles. Go out into it and dig your-

self a bed for the night.'

So Bear went out and began to dig. At first he dug slowly; and then he dug faster and faster and faster with his paws, until there was a huge heap of sand behind him and a great deep hole in front of him. Then Bear lay down in the hole and turned over on his side; and before he knew where he was he had fallen fast asleep. Kind Goat covered him up with sand till only his head was showing, and Bear slept warm and comfortable all through the night, and dreamt some wonderful dreams.

Then Goat went back into the forest and ate some of the fine, fat, juicy brown berries that grow on the bushes there, until she had had enough. She drank some of the sparkling water that ran tinkling down the side of the Marble Mountain through the trees. And then she dug a hole in the sand by Bear's side and lay down in it and went fast off to sleep herself.

II

How Bear and Goat crossed the Great Plain and met Ostrich

BEAR was woken suddenly the next morning by a funny noise going on all round him.

' Maa-aa, maa-aa,' the noise said.

Bear was rather frightened, and pretended he was still asleep. But he looked round him cautiously through half-closed eyelids, and saw that he was surrounded by goats. There were all sorts, sizes, colours and shapes of goat. Old goats, young goats, black goats, white goats, fat goats and thin goats, and all looking very solemn with great curly horns and long, straggly beards which waggled as they bleated. Soon his friend from the night before came prancing up and kicked the sand off his stomach.

' Get up, lazy bones,' said Goat; ' time for breakfast. I'm starting off early to seek my fortune, and these are all my friends and relations who've come to see me off.'

Then Goat butted him playfully in the ribs and pranced off to see that the milk wasn't boiling over.

So Bear got up and ate his porridge with lovely

warm goat's milk poured over it. Then he took
his bell, and licked and gulped until he'd finished
up all the honey inside and it was ready to ring
again when he wanted it.

But Bear was beginning to feel a little jealous
of Goat because, as we know, he was a wandering
sort of Bear. And he'd always wondered what
there was to see beyond the Marble Mountain.

' Are you really going off all alone to seek your
fortune, Goat? ' he said. And when Goat, who
had got her mouth full of berries, nodded, he
asked, ' Are you sure you wouldn't like a little
brown Bear to come with you? '

At that Goat looked very scornful. ' Goats like
walking by themselves,' she said. ' In any case,
what use should I have for a little brown Bear? '

' Well,' said Bear, ' although I'm only a little
Bear as bears go, I'm really very big and strong.
I've got lovely warm brown fur, and I could
cuddle you if you were cold at nights. When you
were sad, I could sing you little songs to cheer you
up. We could play games together and ask each
other riddles. And when you were hungry, I
could go and get you honey from the bees, or
ripe, juicy berries out of the forest.'

That decided Goat, and she nodded gravely
and told Bear he could come; and Bear was so

overjoyed that he ran up and hugged Goat, which is a very difficult thing to do, because goats are such very awkward shapes.

Bear hugged so hard that Goat bleated out 'Let go; you are breaking my bones.' And she was so cross that she nearly told Bear to go home, after all. But Bear shambled off and got her some special juicy berries out of the forest; and so they made it up.

So Bear wrote a message for his mother to tell her he was going off across the plain with Goat to help her seek her fortune; and he gave it to an eagle, who agreed to fly off to the cave near the top of the mountain to deliver it. Goat's mother said she would call in at the cave when she got back to keep Bear's mother company and tell her all about everything. Then, with all her friends and relations bleating and cheering, Goat walked off across the plain towards the sunrise, with Bear trotting by her side.

'We shall walk straight across the plain, leaving the Marble Mountain behind us, until we get to the place we're going to,' said Goat.

'Where are we going to, then?' asked Bear nervously.

'Silly!' answered Goat. 'How shall we know until we get there?'

Goat obviously didn't want to talk. So Bear left her alone, and they walked on for a long time in silence.

As the sun rose higher a mist settled round the Marble Mountain; and when they looked back they couldn't see it behind them any longer. All around them as far as they could see was sand— nothing but sand. They sat down for a time, and hoped the mist would go. But instead it got worse, and Goat began to get impatient.

' We must get on,' she said. ' But how shall we tell which way to go ? '

Bear thought for a little while; and then his thoughts grew into what seemed to him a very good idea. ' I shall put a stick in the ground and mark it with a " one ",' he said. ' Then we shall walk away from the stick until we can't see it any longer. Then I shall put another stick in the ground and mark it with a " two ". Then we shall walk away from that stick until we can't see it any longer. Then I shall . . .'

' Stop,' said Goat, who was afraid Bear might go on for ever. ' I understand. We'll go on doing that till we get to where we're going to. And I only hope we get there soon, because I can't count any higher than twelve.'

So they started off again; and walked a long,

long way; and when Bear had put as
many as nine sticks in the ground, they
could still see nothing but sand all round
them.

Then Goat peered ahead of her and

bleated out ex-
citedly, ' I can
see another
stick! '

' So can I, '
said Bear. ' Some other animal must have been
this way before us.'

They hurried on, and sure enough there was
a stick standing upright in the sand.

Bear looked at it anxiously, and then his face
fell. Notched on the stick in his own great
sprawly handwriting were the letters O-N-E.

Then they realized sadly that for the last two

hours they had been walking round in a great big circle, and had come right back to where they had started from.

❦

Bear sat down in the sand and felt very sad and lonely. The nice warm cave high up near the top of the Marble Mountain seemed very far away. He took up his bell and began ringing it very loudly. But no animals lived out there in the middle of the plain to hear it; or, if there were any animals, none of them took any notice.

Then Goat got very angry. 'You're a fine fellow to take out to seek a fortune,' she said, ' when you ring your bell and want to go home because you get lost on the first day out.'

So Bear looked round him sadly; and as he was looking he thought he saw a Thing. So he looked again, and the Thing was still there. He tapped Goat on the shoulder and pointed. Goat saw the Thing too; and they got up and walked forward until they came to the place where the Thing was.

It was certainly a very peculiar Thing. Two long, spindly legs with long yellow claws on the bottom and a large bunch of feathers on top; and coming out of the bunch of feathers, and going

right down out of sight into the sand, was a long scraggy something which looked as though it might be a neck; but neither of them could imagine any creature with a neck quite so long and scraggy.

They walked round the Thing quietly, looking at it from every angle.

Then Bear coughed politely. 'How do you do, dear sir or madam,' he said.

The Thing didn't move. Then Goat butted it, first gently, and then harder; and still it didn't move.

'I think it must be dead,' said Bear solemnly. 'We shall have to bury it.'

So he started scooping the sand away from round the Thing's neck. And as he scooped first of all a head came to light; and then two beady eyes; and then a long yellow beak. And the creature raised its neck and looked at them through its beady eyes and announced:

'I'm Ostrich; I hoped you wouldn't see me.'

'Dear Ostrich,' said Bear, 'kind Ostrich, can

you tell us the way to the other side of this dreadful plain ? '

' It's not a dreadful plain,' said Ostrich; ' it's a lovely plain. Where else would you find such miles and miles of gorgeous sand ? I come here every Wednesday to get away from the rude animals in the forest, who make fun of me for my long neck. I bury my head in the sand so that nobody can see me, and stay here for twenty-four hours until I feel happy again. It's a lovely plain.'

' I know it's a lovely plain,' said Goat soothingly. ' But I've come out with Bear to seek my fortune, and we want to get to the other side.'

Ostrich looked them up and down; and then said suddenly, ' Come with me '; and started walking off at an enormous pace across the sand.

Goat had to run to keep up with her; and Bear dropped on to all fours and ran too. Ostrich went faster and faster, with her neck stretched forward and her feathers spread out behind her.

' Wait for me,' gasped Bear.

But Ostrich took no notice, and strode on faster and faster still.

Bear and Goat didn't dare to stop and take breath, for fear they might lose sight of her. So they panted on until, just as night was beginning to fall, they walked off the edge of the plain into the heart of a dark forest. And still Ostrich strode on along a broad pathway through the forest, until at long last they came to a clearing. Then Ostrich stopped; and Bear and Goat stopped too, very thankfully, and fell down to rest on the mossy floor of the forest.

' This,' said Ostrich sternly, ' is where we shall build our house.'

' Which house? ' gasped Bear, who had always been inquisitive, ever since he was a cub, and even asked questions in his sleep.

' The house you, me and Goat are going to live in, silly,' retorted Ostrich.

Whereupon she plunged her head into a huge heap of sand; and no amount of butting or prodding could stir her or get another word out of her. So Bear and Goat lay down side by side; and Goat nestled in against Bear's warm brown fur. And they fell into a long, deep sleep, wondering what strange adventures the morning would bring.

III

Ostrich builds a Prefabricated House

BEAR didn't sleep very well that night. There seemed to be a lot of bustle going on around him—animals coming and going and whispering to each other in the darkness. Once he thought he heard a creaking sound like a cart in the distance, and the voice of Ostrich squawking something that sounded like 'Good-bye, Monkeys.' However, in the end he fell off to sleep; and when he woke the sun was quite high above the horizon.

All round him things were happening. A company of beavers with spades on their shoulders were gathered round Ostrich, who was standing on a mound giving them orders.

'Off with your spades to the stream,' Ostrich was saying, 'and build up your dam till the water runs down through the clearing.'

Then the beavers started

asking questions all at once, but they were too far off, and Bear couldn't hear what they were saying. After a bit, however, they fell into line, and marched off through the woods singing the Beaver's song.

In another corner a lot of rabbits were busy burrowing in all directions. And near them a team of badgers was digging trenches. Round an enormous pot a group of animals was dancing hand in hand and singing as they danced:

> *There's always eggs for breakfast when you come*
> *to stay with Ostrich*
> *Ostrich! Ostrich!*
> *Fiddle-diddle-dee.*
> *Boiled eggs, poached eggs, fried eggs, scrambled eggs,*
> *Good old Ostrich!*
> *She's the one for me!*

Ostrich walked over when she saw Bear was awake.

'Hurry up and eat your breakfast,' she said. 'You can have as many eggs as you like. And after that I want you to come and help mix the cement.'

Goat was still asleep; so Ostrich flapped her

wings over her, creating an enormous wind which simply blew Goat awake.

' I'm afraid we're rather short of milk for all these animals, Goat; so would you please give us some of yours? ' said Ostrich. ' And after that I want you to help Bear mix the cement.'

' What's all this about? ' asked Goat drowsily.

' The house we're building,' answered Ostrich.

' I don't want a house,' said Goat, who was often disagreeable in the early morning; ' I'm off to seek my fortune.'

' Silly,' said Ostrich. ' You must have a house first before you start trying to make a fortune. And if you're very good you can put up a brass plate saying " Goat, Fortune-Hunter, lives here ".'

By this time Bear was beginning to get interested. He had already gobbled up three huge Ostrich eggs, and was ready for work.

' What sort of house are we building, Ostrich? ' he asked.

' We're building a prefabricated house,' replied Ostrich.

' And what on earth is that? ' asked Bear.

' It's a house that has been built already,' answered Ostrich. ' You see, it's like this. Far beyond the forest there is a hill; and beyond the hill there is a valley; and in the valley lives Man;

and Man lives in houses.   Man is usually kind to animals; and then we bring him presents and take his children for rides on our backs.   But some men are unkind.   We keep their names on a list; and when each man's turn comes round we send out a cartload of monkeys by dead of night.   The monkeys take his house away as he sleeps; first the chimney-pot, then the roof, and then the walls brick by brick; and then all the furniture except the bed he's sleeping in.   So when the unkind man wakes up in the morning he finds himself all alone in an open field.   We sent the monkeys off last night when you were asleep to bring back the house of a horrid man called Mr Murgatroyd. They ought to be back any moment now.'

And, sure enough, just as Ostrich had finished speaking, four great carts came into sight at the far end of the clearing, each drawn by several big strong monkeys, with a crowd of chattering monkeys riding on top.   The carts were loaded right up with everything you need to make up a house.   There were chimneys and tiles and bricks and doors and windows and a great big knocker to go on the front door, to say nothing of all the chairs and tables and beds and other things to go inside the house when it was built.

The carts drove up to where they were standing

and the monkeys jumped down and started unloading them at once.

✤

As soon as the monkeys had unloaded their carts everything got more and more busy, with Ostrich rushing round, squawking instructions to everybody, and generally getting in the way. Bear and Goat were kept busy mixing the cement. And as soon as the badgers had finished digging the foundations some more animals came and filled them in. Then the beavers finished building their dam, and the water came pouring from the river towards the clearing through the holes the rabbits had dug, and right into the house they were building. The monkeys, who were expert builders, started laying brick upon brick, and the walls rose rapidly from the ground. The monkeys didn't need any scaffolding. They just climbed up and down on each other's backs.

Some older monkeys were busy inside the house
hammering away at the walls and laying the
floors. Later they climbed up, swinging their
hammers to nail the rafters on the roof. When
the walls were up, and the roof was going on, a
flock of parrots flew up, each with a tile in his
beak, and placed it in position on the rafters.
Meanwhile Bear was helping some of the
stronger animals to carry the furniture into the
house and up into the bedrooms; and Goat was
helping to put the china away and the books in
the bookcases.

Everybody worked away with a will, until by
tea-time the great moment came, and Ostrich
climbed up a ladder of monkeys and put the

chimney-pot on top. Then they lit a fire, and smoke puffed out of the chimney. They turned on the taps, and water gushed into the bath. They went around all of the downstairs rooms sitting on each of Mr Murgatroyd's beautiful comfy chairs in turn. Then they went upstairs and bounced up and down on the beds. And while they were doing that, Ostrich had been preparing a huge sit-down tea in the dining-room, with eggs and milk and honey buns and mango jam and an enormous pink cake shaped like a house, with cotton wool to look like smoke coming out of the chimney. The monkeys had found the cake in Mr Murgatroyd's house, and none of the animals had ever seen anything like it before. They all came downstairs for tea; and while they were eating Ostrich called out to a quiet-looking bird sitting in the corner :

' Now, Mr Secretary Bird, you can cross Mr Murgatroyd off your list.'

' What did Mr Murgatroyd do ? ' asked Bear.

' He teased animals,' replied Ostrich. ' He grew lovely juicy things in his garden; and whenever we walked in through the gate to eat them, he jumped out from behind a tree and shouted " Boo! ". He took away cartloads of coco-nuts out of the forest to sell to his greedy friends in the town; and now there are hardly any coco-nut balls left for our children to play with.'

' He was a horrid man,' chanted all the animals sitting round the table.

' But now he hasn't got a house to live in,' continued Ostrich; ' so he'll have to go and live somewhere else, and won't trouble us any more. And now you, Goat, and I have a lovely prefabricated house to live in, haven't we, Bear? '

Bear agreed that it was indeed a lovely house; and even Goat muttered that it wasn't so bad; though, as her mouth was full and she talked through her beard, not all of them heard what she said.

Well, just before the sun set, Ostrich made a little speech thanking everybody for helping to build the house; and somebody called out, ' Three cheers for Ostrich '; and all the animals went off through the forest to their homes. The night fell. The fire blazed up in the hearth; and Bear, Goat and Ostrich felt more snug and cosy than they'd ever felt before. Man might be horrid, they thought; but he did know how to make himself comfortable.

' What shall we call the house? ' said Ostrich.

' We shall call it Mappin Villa,' replied Goat;

and she spoke so firmly that nobody dared to contradict her.

So Mappin Villa it became. And before they went to bed Goat went to the front door and hung up a brass plate saying ' Goat, Fortune-Hunter, lives here.' And Ostrich scribbled a little note underneath in white chalk saying ' So do Bear and Ostrich. No hawkers. No circulars. Please knock and ring. Beware of the Dog.' Outside the door they placed the huge bell, which Bear had carried with him all across the Great Plain, so that anybody who wanted to come in could ring it, if he was strong enough to lift it. And after that they went off to bed and slept right on, between Mr Murgatroyd's lovely clean white sheets, until the middle of the next day.

IV

*Elephant comes to Stay and has to Go;
and Ostrich tells her Story*

BEAR, Goat and Ostrich soon got nicely settled
in. It really was a very comfortable house.
Apart from all the chairs and tables and things,
there were some lovely books, from which they
learnt a lot about some of the nicer things that
Man does. But the best book of all was a simply
splendid book which told them all about a
wonderful thing called cooking, by a woman
called Mrs Beeton. There were one or two bits
in the book about birds and animals that they
didn't like very much, though Bear was quite
interested in the bit about fishes. And there were
lots of things that they were very fond of eating
that Mrs Beeton didn't seem to know about at all,
such as worms and frogs and mice. But the piece
they liked best was the one about buns and cakes
and jellies. Bear used to read it out aloud from
the book while Goat and Ostrich listened, until
they knew it off by heart. Then they would
gather round and look at the pictures until their
mouths began to water. Then Goat would go

into the kitchen and make some lovely things to eat for tea; and they would ask their friends in from the forest and have the most wonderful parties.

There was always plenty to eat at Mappin Villa. Ostrich gave them great big eggs to eat for breakfast. Goat gave them bucketfuls of milk to drink. Bear soon made friends with Mrs Bee. He used to go out and see her every Monday after lunch and come back with lots of jars brimful with honey. With all these things they were able to make the most lovely sticky honey buns, just like the pictures in Mrs Beeton's book. And when Elephant came to tea one day he thought he had never seen such exciting buns in all his life. He picked one up with his trunk, tossed it into the air and caught it in his mouth and swallowed it. He enjoyed doing this so much that he ate one hundred and fifty-three buns, one after the other; and only stopped because there weren't any buns left to eat.

When the sun began to set beyond the Great Plain and behind the Marble Mountain, Elephant got up and said regretfully, ' Well, I really must be going.'

' Must you ? ' said Bear, Goat and Ostrich politely.

' Well, I haven't really got to,' answered Elephant.

So he stayed to supper and ate twenty-three of Ostrich's biggest eggs and drank five bucketfuls of milk. This upset Goat so much that she went into the kitchen and burst into tears. So Ostrich lent her a feather to dry her eyes, and went into the garden to lay some more eggs so that they shouldn't go short for breakfast.

As the moon rose higher and higher over the Marble Mountain, and still Elephant hadn't gone, Bear began to get nervous; and at last he said jokingly :

' It's getting so late, it looks as though we'll have to ask you to stay the night! '

' I don't mind if I do,' replied Elephant, who had heard how comfortable it was at Mappin Villa and thought it would be better than spending a night out in the forest.

Well, of course none of Mr Murgatroyd's beds was nearly big enough for an elephant to sleep in. So they had to make a bed specially for him. It was very difficult. They strapped together five long oak logs from out of the forest. Then they went round to call on Giraffe and borrowed from him some of his special pieces of indiarubber. They were six inches thick, and very strong;

because although it was very clever of Giraffe to write at all, he did it very badly and made lots of spelling mistakes which he had to keep on rubbing out. And he wrote very large letters, because his head was so far away right up on the top of his long neck that otherwise he would never have seen what he was writing. They stuck the pieces of rubber together with some very strong glue and put them on the five oak logs; and there was a fine bed for bouncing on, which they put upstairs in the attic.

It took Elephant a very long time to decide what to do with his trunk. In the end he decided to sleep with it outside the sheets, so that he wouldn't blow the bedclothes off every time he breathed. So by the side of the bed they put a nice comfy sofa so that he would have somewhere to rest

his trunk if he wanted to sleep on his side; and at last all was ready.

By this time, however, Elephant had eaten so much that he had fallen fast asleep in front of the fire. So they got some other animals in to help and carried him upstairs to bed. It wasn't at all easy. They were very tired when they'd finished, and glad to get to bed themselves.

It was a very stormy night inside Mappin Villa. When Elephant breathed in, all the soot came down the chimney. When he breathed out, the roof jumped up three inches in the air. And when he started snoring, the whole house shook; and all the little mice jumped in their little skins and rushed out into the forest for safety. They were all very glad when the morning came.

Well, after breakfast the next morning, Elephant said, ' I really must be going now! '

' Must you? ' asked Bear, Goat and Ostrich politely.

' Well, I haven't really got to,' answered Elephant.

So he stayed for lunch. And so it went on from meal to meal and from day to day, until Bear, Goat and Ostrich got thoroughly tired of making honey buns and watching Elephant eat them. Besides, every time he laughed, or leant against

the wall, they were afraid the house would fall
down.   And they wondered how they would ever
get him to go.

⁂

One Monday afternoon, when Bear was visiting
his friend Mrs Bee to collect the honey, he told
her all their troubles with Elephant.

' It's not as though he isn't very kind and nice,'
said Bear; ' but there's so much of him.   And he
simply doesn't know when to go.'

Mrs Bee listened sympathetically, and then
said, ' You leave it all to me.'

Later that afternoon, as Elephant was sleeping
out in the garden after a lunch of one hundred and
seventy-five large honey buns, there was a buzzing
noise in the distance.   It grew nearer and nearer,
and the sky grew darker and darker, as a huge
swarm of the buzziest sort of busy bee approached.
One lot of bees settled all over Elephant and
started tickling him; whilst another swarm flew
round and round ten yards in front of his trunk
buzzing as they flew ' Bunz, Bunz.'

Elephant rushed round and round the garden
and out through the gate following the sound of
' Bunz,' while the other bees tickled and tickled
and tickled.   Bear, Goat and Ostrich peeped out
anxiously from behind the curtains.

Then the bees, still buzzing away and saying 'Bunz, Bunz, Bunz,' flew off down the road and Elephant rushed after them, laughing and squirming as the bees tickled him.

So Bear, Goat and Ostrich put the roof back on the house and mended the springs in all the chairs Elephant had sat in. They tied some old feathers that Ostrich didn't want any more on to the end of a long stick and swept the chimney, and got everything clean and tidy once more.

Then they hung up a large notice in the window written in elephant language and saying ' No buns to-day '. And every elephant who passes by looks at the window, reads the notice, shakes his trunk sadly and walks on into the forest where the mangoes grow.

❧

As they were sitting round the fire the evening after Elephant had left, Bear suddenly turned to Ostrich and said, ' Now that we've got the place to ourselves again, tell us something about yourself and what you did before we met you and how you got this splendid idea of living in a house.'

' My story is very complicated,' said Ostrich. ' But, as you know, I'm rather a silly bird, and always forget everything almost as soon as it's happened to me. So there isn't much I can tell you.

' My mother ran away when I was very young. She was always a great runner. I take after her,' said Ostrich proudly. ' But one day she ran too far. Some unkind Man caught her and took her far away across the sea and put her in a place they call the Zoo. I didn't know this at the time, and wandered off a long way looking for her, until I came to this forest, which is far away from where all the other ostriches live.'

' What is the sea ? ' asked Goat, interrupting.

' I don't know,' answered Ostrich. ' But they tell me that it is always very wet. If you really want to know you'll have to ask the fishes, if you can understand what they say and can get them to talk to you. Whenever I try to talk to them, they just make funny faces at me and swim away.'

' And what happens in this Zoo they talk about ? ' asked Bear.

' I have been told,' answered Ostrich; ' but I've forgotten most of it, and what I remember always rather frightens me. But I believe there are lots of other birds and animals there and they nearly all live in houses. My mother lives in a very important place called the Ostrich House.

' I'm told it's a very comfortable house,' Ostrich went on, ' and there's plenty of good food. Man comes into the Zoo every day so that the animals can have something to look at. But Man is very ugly and it must be rather dull.'

' It sounds horrible to me,' said Bear, ' in spite of the food. How do you know all this ? '

' I know it from the swallows,' said Ostrich. ' Once a year, when the winter is coming, they fly away across the sea. Some of them always go and visit my mother and tell her all the news.

And when they come back in the spring they bring me messages from her.'

' Haven't you found it rather lonely here? ' asked Bear.

' It's been very lonely,' said Ostrich. ' You see, there are lots of all the other sorts of bird and animal in the forest, and they like to go about together. But there's only one of me. So it's lovely having the two of you to live with me, because you're the only Bear and Goat in the forest, just as I'm the only Ostrich. And I've always wanted to live in a house, because the house my mother lives in sounds as if it would be so nice if only it wasn't so far away and in the Zoo.'

' I certainly shouldn't like to live in a house in the Zoo,' said Bear. ' It must be horrid not being able to go out whenever you want to.'

' Anything to do with Man is horrid,' said Goat, with a shudder.

' Except the food in Mrs Beeton's Cookery Book,' added Bear; and he went up to bed to dream about it.

V

Goat tells her Story

THE next night, as Bear was warming his paws,
and Goat was warming her hooves, and
Ostrich was warming her claws before a great,
big, crackling fire, Ostrich suddenly said to Goat,
' And what made you wander off down the Marble
Mountain and across the plain and into the
forest?' Because Ostrich was a very inquiring
sort of bird, and always liked to know where everybody was and why they were there.

' Mine is a very sad story,' said Goat.

She borrowed a feather from Ostrich to wipe a
tear from her eye, waggled her beard gravely, and
began.

' One day I wandered away from my father and
mother far away down the other side of the
Marble Mountain. I was chasing a butterfly;
and the butterfly went on and on and on; until it
flew across the river and I lost it. Then I came
to a field; and round the field was a hedge;
and in the hedge was a gate; and the gate was
open. So I walked in; and the hedge was thick

with the biggest, brownest, juiciest berries I have
ever met; and I ate and ate and ate.

' I must have fallen asleep. Because when I
woke up a woman was standing over me. She
had a bucket in one hand and a stool in the other;
and before I knew what was happening she sat
down by my side on her stool and drew off all my
milk into her bucket. You can guess how angry
I was.

' When she got up and left, I tried to follow her
out of the field. But I hadn't gone far before
something tugged at my neck; and I found I was
tied on to the end of a rope, the other end of which
was fixed into the ground, right in the middle of the
field and far far away from that lovely hedge.

' So it went on for days and days. Every
morning and every afternoon the woman came
into the field with her bucket and her silly little
stool and milked me. Oh, the shame of it! To
turn me, a free Goat from the Marble Mountain,
into a domesticated animal, just like any stupid
cow! Every day I would bleat at her " Maa-aa,
maa-aa; I can't reach the hedge." But she took
no notice; and walked off with her bucket full of
my milk, leaving me alone there in the middle of
the field, with nothing but grass to eat.

' One day, however, she was going out for a

walk with the farmer's son; or so I understood, for she sang songs about him as she milked me. She left in a great hurry; and very carelessly left the gate of my field open.

' In the field next to me lived a creature called Horse. I had never seen him, because the hedge was too high; but we used to call out to each other sometimes, and had got quite friendly. Although he was only a domesticated animal, he was quite interesting to talk to, and knew a lot of riddles.

' Well, Horse was taking a stroll round his field after his lunch, and was very surprised to find the gate open. He hesitated a little, and then came through the gate into my field. He looked around him for a while, and then trotted straight up to me. So I looked at him and said " Maa-aa, maa-aa; I can't reach the hedge; " and then I put my head on one side and waggled my beard at him in a friendly way.

' To my horror, the creature sat down in front of me and laughed and laughed and laughed. I suppose I ought to have forgiven him, be- cause he had never seen a goat before, and was only a very young Horse. But I was very angry. There I was in the middle of a field with a rope round my neck, and a lovely hedge right away out of my reach, and nothing happening but a silly woman coming into my field twice a day to milk me. I felt I had enough troubles, without stupid domesticated animals coming into my field and sitting down and laughing at me. So I put my head down, and took a run and butted that rude Horse very hard. He whinnied with fright, and jumped up and started bolting away as fast as he could go; and I kept my head down and ran after him. But just as I was going to butt him again I felt a sharp tug on my neck, and found I had come to the end of my rope. The creature sat down at a safe distance and laughed and laughed; and when he got tired

of that he got up and strolled away out of the field, chuckling to himself as he went. By this time I didn't mind what happened to me. I lay down and put my head between my hooves and cried and cried and cried. I told you it was a very sad story.'

By this time Goat's eyes were wet with tears; and Bear and Ostrich were feeling very sad, too, and kept on saying ' boo-hoo ' to show how sorry they were for her. However, Goat bravely dried her tears away with her beard and went on.

*

' I cried for a long time,' said Goat. ' When I looked up at last, I saw Horse standing in front of me again. I made up my mind to butt him really hard this time, so that he wouldn't forget me in a hurry. But there he was, speaking very kindly and saying how very sorry he was. I found out later that his mother had spoken to him very sharply for being rude to me. So I said to him " Maa-aa maa-aa; I can't reach the hedge."

' " Don't worry," he said to me; " you shall reach the hedge."

' Then he walked away to the other end of my rope, where it was fixed into the ground; and with two great kicks of his strong hind legs he kicked it out, and I was free.

' Well, of course I ran straight across to the hedge and started eating all the lovely juicy berries I'd been looking at from the end of my rope for so long. They were much riper and lovelier than I had remembered.

' When I had eaten my fill I went back to Horse, who was sitting there waiting for me, and thanked him for being so kind. He was really a most amiable Horse, when you got to know him. We walked round the field talking; and when we came to the gate the woman had left open we walked through it into the next field, and he took me up to meet his mother. She was a most charming animal, and at once asked me to stay to tea; and as they were rather short of milk, I gave them some of mine to help. We had a lovely tea, though the food was rather horsey for me, and I was already full up with berries. But suddenly, just as I was eating my last bagful of oats, a gate opened in the end of the field near the farmhouse; and into the field came that dreadful woman with her silly little stool and her beastly bucket.

' I felt certain she would see me and lead me back into the next field and tie me up again. But Horse's mother quickly galloped towards her across the field, whinnying and tossing her mane as she went, and frightened the woman so much that she dropped her bucket and stool and ran away out of the field the way she'd come in. While his mother was doing this, Horse kicked away at the ground with his strong hind legs until he had dug a great big hole. " Into the hole, quickly," he cried excitedly. So I jumped in, and he covered me up with twigs and leaves, so that no one would ever have thought there was a goat there at all.

' We weren't troubled again that night; and we sat up together for a long time, telling each other stories and playing guessing games. I had a lovely long sleep, and in the morning had a glorious breakfast off the berries in the hedge.

' But as we were sitting and talking after break-fast, suddenly the gate opened and the woman came into the field with two big men. I quickly jumped into the hole, and kind Horse and his mother covered me with twigs and leaves again. The woman came straight across the field and stopped just near my hole. I hardly dared to breathe.

' " That's the horse," I heard her say. " She ran after me across the field last night and frightened me very badly. You'll have to send her away and sell her."

' These cruel people went on talking together

for a bit; and after a while, peeping out through
the twigs, I saw them put a rope round the necks of
poor kind Horse and his mother and lead them
away out of the field. I didn't even have a chance
to say good-bye. I was all alone in the world
again.

' Then the woman came back with her silly
stool and her beastly bucket and walked across the
field right past the hole in which I was hiding and
into the field next door. I heard her in the
distance calling out " Nanny, nanny, nanny! "
in her silly, squeaky voice.

' After a bit she gave it up and went back into
the farmhouse; and I was glad she was going to
have to go without milk that day.

' I thought things over to myself and decided I
had got to escape. It wasn't going to be easy,
as all the gates were shut and the hedge was very
thick. As soon as the sun was down I came out of
my hole and walked over to the far hedge. The
forest was on the other side. I ate and ate
steadily for three hours, and by that time I had
eaten myself half-way through the hedge. I had
to rest for a while. But soon I was eating again.
By the time the sun rose I was nearly through.

' I went on eating. Then suddenly I glanced
over my shoulder and saw that dreadful woman

coming into the field again. She saw me almost at once, and started shouting " Nanny, nanny, nanny," and running towards me. But she was too late. One last enormous bite, and I was able to scramble through on to the other side of the hedge into the forest.

' Then I ran and ran and ran for miles and miles, until I was quite sure the woman wasn't following me. I was so full of all the hedge I had eaten, and so tired with all my running, that I lay down and slept for all the rest of the day and right through the next night.

' That night I had a dream. A fairy appeared to me and said to me " Go forth, Goat, and seek your fortune." So when I woke I went back up the Marble Mountain to see my father and mother and all my brothers and sisters. I said good-bye to them all and set out. I wandered off down the side of the mountain; and when I came to the edge of the plain, I met Bear.'

Goat stopped talking. The fire had burnt very low. So she kicked it with one of her hooves, and it flickered and burst into flame.

Bear woke up with a start. ' What a very sad story,' he said. ' It only shows that the less you have to do with Man, the better. Ostrich and I will plant a hedge to-morrow morning right round the house, so that you'll always have something near you to eat when you're hungry.'

' What a horrid woman! ' said Ostrich. ' What was her name? '

' Well,' said Goat, ' I don't really know. But I heard one of the men call her " crosspatch ", so perhaps that was her name.'

' A very suitable name,' remarked Ostrich. ' Miss Crosspatch! I shall get the Secretary Bird to put it on our list. You never know when we might want another prefabricated house.'

' A good idea,' said Goat; ' I like to think of her waking up one morning and finding herself all alone in the middle of a field. Serve her right! '

After which they all three yawned, said good night to each other, took their candles and went upstairs to bed.

VI

Owl comes to Stay and Bear finds he likes Birds after all

THE house was very quiet after Elephant had left. But it also seemed very empty; and Bear, Goat and Ostrich decided that it was rather lonely.

'There aren't any very good games for three,' said Bear one night. ' We shall have to find some other animal to come and play with us.'

So Ostrich sent for the Secretary Bird. ' He's our Civil Servant,' she explained. ' He does all the writing for us, and keeps lists, and sends out forms for us to fill in. We don't take much notice of what he says, and most of us can't read or write anyway; but he comes in very useful sometimes. He uses such lovely long words.'

' Isn't he a very lonely bird? ' asked Bear.

' Not really,' answered Ostrich. ' He sits all day on a fine branch near the top of a very large tree. He's very clever, and they keep on moving him up to a higher branch. They say he'll get to the top of the tree one day. And he has a very jolly time writing letters to other Secretary Birds on different branches of his tree or on other trees in the same clump.   He doesn't talk very much; but they say he's always thinking; and that makes him very happy.'

So the Secretary Bird came in to see them one night on his way home from the tree where he went to work.   He listened very solemnly to what they had to say; nodded; and said, ' Leave it to, your obedient servant.'

The next day a number of very young Secretary Birds flew round the forest fixing on the trees a notice which said:

> ' Wanted: gentle animal to play games with Bear, Goat and Ostrich.   Animals that bark and bite need not apply.'

Well, they got lots and lots of answers; and they asked all the animals who had answered to come and see them on the next wet Thursday afternoon, to find out if they liked their faces.

Rhinoceros was the first one to come; and of course they couldn't even pretend to like his face. Nobody does.   So he had to go away again back to the swamp by the river.

After him there came along in turn a sea-lion, a giraffe, a dormouse, a Shetland pony, a hedge-hog and a monkey.

The sea-lion came barking in through the front door, splashing water all over the carpet, and they told him to go away at once, because they didn't want to have anything to do with animals that barked. Bear didn't mind; but it made Goat and Ostrich nervous, and when Ostrich was nervous her feathers used to fall out. The sea-lion said that he didn't bite and could play ludo, hunt the slipper, and the mouth-organ. But that wasn't good enough, so he had to go.

The giraffe was very kind. But when he sat downstairs in the sitting-room, he had to put his head out through the window or up the chimney because the ceiling was so low. They decided it would be difficult to play games like that because they'd always have to be going out of doors or up on to the roof

to find out what he was saying, and then back indoors to see which card he'd played. So that wasn't any good, either.

The dormouse was very sweet and cuddly; and Bear stroked him while Ostrich asked him questions. But after two minutes he had fallen fast asleep, and nothing they could do would wake him. So they stopped an elderly monkey who was passing the house and  asked her to take Dormouse home and give him back to his mother, which she did. They never saw him again so it's quite possible that he's still asleep.

The Shetland pony was a very jolly animal who had wandered into the forest from the town nearby; but apparently he was only good at

horse-play. He had a little horse-play with Bear and Goat; and by the time they had broken three cups and had knocked the picture of Goat's grandmother off the mantelpiece, Ostrich decided that they'd had enough. So they gave him a bundle of hay to eat and sent him off home.

The hedgehog turned out to be a most disagreeable fellow—full of pricks and bristles. Goat thought a hedgehog might come in useful for combing her beard, which was getting very untidy. But Hedgehog insisted that if he came to stay with them he would have to sleep on the pillow in Bear's bed. They had seen Bear with a sore head once before, and they didn't want to again. So Hedgehog was asked to go, and he walked out of the house muttering angrily.

The monkey was a very cheeky creature. He came into the room juggling with two coco-nuts, and Bear thought it was the cleverest thing he'd ever seen. Then Monkey walked across to Ostrich and pulled a knife and  fork out from under one of her feathers. Goat bleated with laughter. They decided monkey was just the sort of creature they wanted, and they asked him to sit down and play a game of Snakes and Ladders. But he ran off and climbed up the curtains, and jumped off on to the grandfather clock, and from there on to the mantelpiece; and it was a long time before they could persuade

him to sit down at all. Then, just as the game was getting really exciting, Monkey knocked the board over. He thought this was frightfully funny; but nobody else did. They decided he was a tiresome animal and wouldn't do, after all.

And when he started teasing Ostrich and pulling feathers out of her, Bear decided they'd had enough of the cheeky creature. He picked him up and threw him out of the window; and as he ran away into the forest Bear threw his two coco-nuts after him.

❧

Just as they were beginning to wonder if they'd ever get a nice, friendly animal to play with them, there was a hooting noise outside, and a great brown Owl flew through the window and perched on top of the grandfather clock.

The very thought of hedgehog was giving Bear a sore head. So he grunted, ' Go away. We advertised for an animal. We don't want any silly birds.'

Ostrich was very angry about this. She strutted about the room squawking and flapped her feathers so fiercely that everything blew off the mantelpiece into the fireplace. ' I think it would be very nice to have another bird in the house,' she said. 'I'm tired of all these conceited animals with all their silly fur. Give me feathers every time.'

Owl raised his eyebrows and looked at them all very solemnly. ' Why,' he asked, ' is a goat like the afternoon? '

They all puzzled and puzzled and puzzled.

'Because it's got a beard,' said Bear after a while.

' Silly! ' replied Owl. ' Who ever heard of an afternoon with a beard? '

They had one or two other tries, but in the end they had to give it up.

So Owl told them, ' A goat is like the afternoon because they both end with tea.'

Well, they thought that was a splendid riddle; and Owl told them some more. And in the end, even Bear had to admit that he was a fine fellow, even though he was only a bird. He was so wise. He not only knew all the games they knew, but taught them lots of new ones, like noughts and crosses and beggar-my-neighbour. Besides, he was so good at organizing things.

So Owl came to stay. And they made him up a lovely bed out on the roof behind the chimney-stack to keep him warm and shelter him from the cold north winds.

There was a little trouble at first because Owl was a nocturnal creature. But when he learnt of all the lovely things they did in the day time, he agreed to change his habits and see how he got on.

So every morning, just before the sun rose, Owl used to fly off to get worms for his breakfast. He had to eat them raw, because there was nothing in Mrs Beeton to tell him how to cook them. When he came back he would tell them all the news of the forest. How Mrs Badger was going to have a baby again; and Tommy Tiger had got measles; and how the monkeys had been down into the town and had come back wearing a lot of funny hats, and nobody knew where they'd got them from.

Now, when Ostrich saw Owl flying around she got very jealous, and said, ' What's the use of these great big wings of mine if I can't fly, too? ' So she got out of the window and climbed up on to the roof, and gave a great big squawk, and flapped her wings and jumped.

Owl was annoyed because she always landed in a heap on the flower-beds where he planted all the seeds that he brought back from his visits to the gardens in the town. But Bear thought it was the funniest thing he'd ever seen in his life. He stood up in the garden holding his sides and nearly burst with laughter. And when he couldn't stand 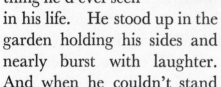 up any longer, he lay down on the grass and rolled over and over and over. Because he was always telling Ostrich that she wasn't really a bird at all.

Then, when Ostrich got tired of trying to fly, she would go away and bury her head in the sand. Then Bear and Goat and all the other animals used to go and play leapfrog over her back, while Ostrich went on trying to pretend they hadn't seen her, and kind Owl stayed at home and got the lunch ready.

And every afternoon they had fun. And every evening they had games. And now, if you ask Bear, he'll tell you that he thinks birds are simply splendid, especially owls.

VII

Goat goes seeking her Fortune

AFTER they'd all been together for a week or
so, Goat started behaving in a very funny way.
When all the other animals went out to play, Goat
would go upstairs to her bedroom. There she
would sit at the window for hours on end looking
out into the distance and sighing. Then she
started going out for long walks into the forest all
by herself, carrying lots of big balls of string on her
horns.

Owl was very fond of Goat, and began to get
worried. One day he flew after her very quietly,
taking great care to keep hidden behind the trees,
to find out what she was doing. He found Goat
had tied one end of a ball of string round a tree,
and was looking up to see where the sun was.
Then she marched slowly forward away from the
sun counting aloud, with the ball of string on her
horns unwinding as she went. When she had
counted up to fifty she stopped, looked around her
and started digging. She dug for an hour and
made a very big hole indeed. But she didn't

seem at all satisfied with what she'd done.
' There's nothing in it,' she said shaking her head
sadly; and walked off to a place where there was a
lot of sand and started drawing funny patterns
with her hooves.

Goat looked so very unhappy that kind Owl
couldn't stand it any longer. He flew up very
quietly and perched on the bough of a tree just
over Goat's head. ' Tu whu,' said Owl nervously.

Goat took no notice at all, and went on drawing
her patterns in the sand.

' Tu whit, tu whu,' said Owl, a little more
loudly.

Goat still took no notice.

' Tu whit, tu whit, tu whit, tu whu,' said Owl,
very firmly.

Goat started and looked up. ' Whatever are
you doing here? ' she bleated angrily. ' I'm not
going to have any birds flying round and spying
on me.'

Owl didn't say anything. But he flew down
and drew two straight lines in the sand and two
more straight lines across them. In the square
in the middle he drew a nought. Then he
turned to Goat. ' Your turn,' he said.

Now, if there was one thing Goat couldn't
resist, it was a good game of noughts and crosses.

She walked over and drew her cross. Goat won
that game. She won the next game, too; and
the one after that. Owl let her go on winning
because winning always made Goat happy. After
a bit she had forgotten all about her grumpiness and
was laughing and bleating away just like the old
Goat all the birds and animals in the forest were
so fond of. Then Owl took her and showed her a
place in the forest where there were great bunches
of ripe juicy berries to eat. They got talking about
things, and finally Owl asked Goat what had
happened to her, and why she had been behaving
in such a funny way.

At first Owl thought she wasn't going to answer.
And when she did start speaking, she spoke very
rapidly in goat language which Owl didn't
understand. ' Maa-maa! maa-maa! ' said
Goat.

So Owl raised his eyebrows and looked at Goat
very solemnly. ' Why,' he asked, ' is your skin
like the sun? '

Goat stopped bleating and started thinking.
But in the end she had to give it up.

' Because it's got you(u) in it,' answered Owl.

Goat bleated with laughter. ' You're a good
sort, Owl,' she said. ' And I'm sorry I've been so
rude and grumpy. But, you see, I've been

seeking my fortune. I've been looking for it all over the forest for days and days and days, and I can't find it anywhere.'

' Well, I'm blessed,' said Owl. ' Whatever put such funny ideas into your head ? '

' It's not a funny idea,' said Goat. ' It's a very good idea. It must be, because I saw it in a book. The woman who milked me when I was a prisoner in the field always brought a book with her, and I used to look over my shoulder at the pictures. There was a man in the book. He did just what I've been doing. He used to draw maps in the sand and tie pieces of string round trees. Then he used to walk away from the sun counting, and when he stopped he dug. He was always finding fortunes that way. I've learnt to count,' added Goat proudly. ' I could never go beyond twelve before, but now I can count up to one hundred and twenty-three.'

' Why one hundred and twenty-three ? ' asked Owl.

' Because that's as far as I can go,' answered Goat. ' I've been sitting at my bedroom window morning after morning practising my counting when the other animals went out to play.'

' Well, well, well,' said Owl. ' And how do you know which tree to tie the string round and how far to count before you stop walking away from it, and where to start digging?'

'Alas!' said Goat, 'that's just what I don't know; and that's what makes it all so difficult. I couldn't really tell everything from the pictures in the book, especially as they were upside down. And, in any case, one day when I was very hungry I snatched the book out of the woman's hands and ate it before she could stop me. I don't expect I'll ever find out now.'

'And what is a fortune like when you do find it?' asked Owl.

'I've really got no idea at all,' answered Goat. 'And they tell me nobody knows at first when he's found his fortune. But I'm hoping that mine will be something soft and pink.'

'It sounds like a blancmange to me,' thought Owl. But, being a wise old bird, he didn't say it.

✣

'Well, well,' said Owl at last, 'it's getting far too late to seek any more fortunes to-day. We'd better get back home to Mappin Villa and have some tea.'

So Goat sighed, and put the balls of string on her horns and walked sadly back to Mappin Villa, with Owl flying overhead asking her riddles to try to cheer her up.

When they got back Goat gave them some of her milk to drink as usual; but said she didn't want to have any tea herself, and went upstairs to bed.

When Goat had gone, Owl told Bear and Ostrich to come close, and whispered to them all he had found out about her.

'It's very sad,' he said. 'You see, Goat was brought up on top of a mountain, and never went to school, like Ostrich and me. So she keeps on getting silly ideas into her head, like this one about her fortune. I'm afraid she won't be happy till she finds it, or thinks she has, and we three have got to help her.'

'I'm afraid I never went to school, either, and I'm very ignorant, too,' said Bear humbly. 'What is a fortune, and how does one find it?'

'Cackle, cackle,' said Ostrich, surprisingly; 'my face is my fortune.'

Bear roared with laughter. 'Have you ever seen your face?' he asked.

'No, never,' said Ostrich. 'I've often wondered what it looks like. Sometimes I run round very quickly in a circle in the hope of catching it up and getting a glimpse of it, but I have not managed to yet. And every time I get near a piece of water and try to look at my face in it, the monkeys come up and throw stones into the water and splash about and make waves. They say it would be bad for me to know how beautiful I am.'

' Don't worry, Ostrich,' said Owl. ' We all like your face, even if it is rather funny. And you've got the loveliest feathers of any bird in the forest.'

Ostrich blushed with pride and pleasure.

' Fortunes aren't found at the top of trees,' Owl went on; ' nor by digging deep holes in the sand. True fortune is to be happy and healthy and to have lots of good, kind friends.'

' Then I've found my fortune,' said Bear; ' because everybody is always very kind to me; and I couldn't be happier than I am now, living here with you and Goat and Ostrich.'

' That's right,' said Owl. ' The fairy told Goat in her dream to go forth and seek her fortune. And she found it when she met you and Ostrich and came to live in Mappin Villa. But, as Goat says, nobody knows at first when he's found his fortune. He may go on looking long after he's really found it.'

' We shall have to help Goat,' said Ostrich. ' We can't leave her wandering about like this, looking more like a Ghost than a Goat.'

'There's only one thing for it,' said Owl. 'We shall have to organize an expedition.'

'How gorgeous!' cried out Bear and Ostrich together, and started jumping up and down with excitement.

'Quiet, creatures!' ˙snapped Owl severely. 'You'll wake Goat. Leave it to me to think things over, and I'll let you know my plans at breakfast.'

Then Owl flew out of the window and up on to the roof to his bed behind the chimney-stack; and there he perched for hours and hours and hours, with his wings folded across his chest and his eyes half shut, thinking and thinking and thinking, until the sun rose, when he flew off in a great hurry, in case he should be too late to catch any early worms for his breakfast.

VIII

The Great Expedition begins

A T breakfast next morning Owl explained his plans to Goat, and Goat bounced up and down with excitement like an indiarubber ball. 'You dear, good, kind Owl,' she bleated.

'You'll have to be very patient,' said Owl. 'I shall fly away as soon as I've washed up the breakfast. And I shall go on flying until I come to a nice, likely place to start looking for fortunes. Then I'll fly back to Mappin Villa and we'll all go off together and look. I may be away a very long time.'

So after breakfast, and when they'd finished the washing up, Owl flew out of the window and away over the tree-tops; and they stood waving to him until he disappeared into the distance. Then Bear and Ostrich got busy organizing fun and games to keep Goat happy until Owl came back.

Owl was away for three whole days and two whole nights; and they began to wonder if he'd got lost and if they would ever see him again. Then just as the sun was setting at the end of the third day, and they were sitting down to supper, there was a hoot outside, and Owl came flying in through the window and perched on the grandfather clock.

'Guess where I've been,' said Owl.

'None of your riddles, please,' said Goat impatiently. 'Let's hear your story at once.'

'Well,' said Owl, 'I flew away over the forest, and over the place where Man lives, and over the fields beyond, until I came to a very high hill. Then it was night, and I went to sleep. When the sun rose I flew up to the top of the hill, and saw below me a broad, rich valley bathed in sunshine. Suddenly, far off in the distance, I saw a most extraordinary animal. I flew nearer to have a look at it. It was a very large and very long animal, and it ran very fast and very straight. As it ran it breathed out great clouds from its nostrils; and all the time it ran it said " Choof-choo-oof-choof-choof," and " Jiggety-jig, jiggety-jig." Suddenly it gave a loud hoot and disappeared into a hole in the earth. It was certainly the strangest animal I've ever seen, and I was rather frightened. So I went a little way off to look for worms; and although it was midday, I found hundreds and hundreds of the fattest, juiciest worms I have ever tasted.'

' Were there some berries there? ' asked Goat.

' There were big, brown, juicy berries on every bush,' answered Owl. ' And the bees made such a hum buzzing around collecting honey from all the flowers that you could hardly hear yourself think.

' Well,' continued Owl, ' as I was eating worms, another animal, or perhaps it was the same animal, came out of the hole in the ground, running the other way, and going very, very fast indeed. It puffed away across the valley between the trees until it was out of sight. This happened twice again before sunset; and I found that the animal ran on long, straight lines and never left them; so it was safe to come quite close to it. That night the animal came running past me again. It was all lit up from end to end, and its head seemed to be on fire. It was really rather terrifying for me out there all alone. I thought things over, and decided that a place with such a wonderful animal living in it, and with such lovely worms and berries and so many bees, must be just the place to look for a fortune. So I decided to fly away and come straight back to Mappin Villa and fetch you all.'

' It sounds a very frightening place indeed for a nervous bird like me,' said Ostrich. ' I shouldn't

like to go there unless there's lots and lots of sand
for me to hide in.'

'The place is full of sand,' said Owl.   'Where
it comes from, don't ask me.   But there it is.
Worms, berries, bees and sand and that wonderful
animal.   What more could we want.   We shall
start off straight away.'

Ostrich got up and powdered her beak, and
smoothed out her feathers.   'I'm ready,' she said.

'Stupid!' said Owl.   'We're going to be away
for a long time, and there are lots of things we shall
have to collect to take with us.   We'll all start
working now;   then we'll have a little sleep;   and
we'll start off as soon as the sun rises.'

'Don't forget the tickets,' said Bear.

'What are "tickets"?' asked Goat.

'I haven't the faintest idea,' answered Bear.   'I
only know it's a thing everybody has to say when
he's going on a journey.'

⁂

They were ready to start at dawn.   Bear had
a huge bag full of all the things they thought they
might want on the journey, including Mrs
Beeton's wonderful book about cooking.

Lots of other animals had gathered to cheer,
and Owl and Goat made little speeches.   Bear

promised to bring back presents for all the animals; and Ostrich promised to bring back presents for all the birds.

' Don't forget the tickets,' they all said, so as to be sure they were doing the right thing; and off they walked into the forest.

Goat was so excited she kept rushing on ahead, and Owl had to fly after her and tell her to wait for the others. In the end Bear, who was getting rather hot and grumpy, made her carry the bag on her back; and that slowed her down a lot. They had a lovely lunch in the middle of the forest; then they pushed on until half an hour before sunset, when they came to the forest's edge. Owl told them to be very, very quiet, so that Man shouldn't hear them. They hid behind trees and peered out cautiously.

There ahead of them was a green field. Beyond the field the land sloped down into a broad valley. Through the valley ran a great, winding, silvery river. And on either side of the river were hundreds and thousands of little red-roofed houses, each of them just like Mappin Villa, with little puffs of smoke coming out of their chimneys and curling up lazily into the evening air.

' Oo-oo,' said Bear, who had never seen anything so exciting in all his life.

' Sh! stupid! ' hissed Owl; ' Man will hear you.'

And as he spoke a lot of children came running by across the field, laughing and shouting as they ran. Bear longed to run out and hug them, they looked so happy and jolly; but Goat and Ostrich grabbed hold of his fur and held him back.

Slowly the sun set; and as it got darker the lights went on in the streets and in the windows of all the little houses, and their reflections danced and sparkled in the waters of the big, broad river like thousands of little stars.

Far away they heard a clock strike ' nine '. They went on waiting; and as it got later and later the lights of the town went out one by one. As the clock in the distance struck ' twelve ' Owl fluttered down beside them and whispered : ' Follow me! '

They followed Owl across the field and down the hill and through the silent streets of the town. Ostrich went first, with her head poked forward and her feathers tucked into a pair of knickers, in case they fluttered with fright and woke somebody up. Goat came next, trotting along very stealthily. And Bear came padding along softly behind them, carrying the big bag and grunting to himself with excitement.

Once a dog started barking at them as they crept by, but Owl flew at him fiercely and frightened him into silence. All the cats who were walking round the streets paused in amazement to see them go by; then carried on searching for fishes' heads in the dustbins. They came to a big white bridge over the river; and bending low, so that nobody should see them, ran quickly across to the other side.

On they went. As they passed one house they heard a little boy crying out, ' Mummy, look! There's a bear, a goat and an ostrich walking past our house! ' A light went on upstairs and they heard his mother saying, ' Don't talk nonsense, you silly boy. You're dreaming ! '

They hurried on keeping close to the wall.

Just as they were coming to the edge of the town, and thought they were safe, they heard a ' tramp tramp tramp ' noise.

' Somebody's coming,' muttered Goat.

' Oh dear! Oh dear! ' moaned Ostrich; ' I'm sure somebody will catch us and put us in the Zoo.'

Owl flew down at them. ' Run, run,' he hooted.

Off they rushed down the street. As they ran they heard somebody shouting after them. But on they rushed, making a tremendous noise, with

Ostrich squawking and Goat bleating, and Bear grunting with the weight of the bag he was carrying and Owl hooting to cheer them on.

Soon they were out of the town and on their way across the fields. But still they went on running and running for miles and miles, until they came to the hill Owl had told them about. They climbed and climbed until they came to the top; and just as they got there the sun rose.

'There!' said Owl, pointing proudly ahead of him.

And sure enough, far away across the valley they saw little puffs of white smoke, just as he had told them; and a long snakelike thing running very fast and very straight. And as they listened they heard in the distance, carried on the morning breeze, a voice saying 'Choof-choo-oof-choof-choof; jiggety-jig, jiggety-jig.'

' Wonderful! ' said Goat wearily, ' but I'm afraid it will have to wait. I'm going to sleep.'

Bear and Ostrich had gone to sleep already. So Owl left them, and flew off to find some worms for his breakfast.

IX

They meet a Remarkable Animal and go for a Ride

BEAR, Goat and Ostrich were woken up soon after noon by an enormous hoot. They found Owl had gathered a lot of sticks together and had lit a lovely, crackling fire. He had got their lunch laid out on the grass ready to eat, and a kettle boiling away.

' Get up, you lazy creatures,' Owl hooted.

So they rose and yawned and stretched themselves, and sat down and had a lovely lunch. At the end they had some gorgeous wobbly red jellies, which Owl had made for them as a special treat. Ostrich was particularly fond of jelly. She thought it was the nicest of all the things in Mrs Beeton's book. She loved to swallow it whole and feel it slipping all the way down inside her long neck. It was a real picnic. The food was all on the ground, and they ate with their finger or claws, or just dug their snouts or their beaks into it. So there was no washing up; and as soon as they'd finished they set off down the hill.

Owl flew on ahead to show them the way. Goat was jumping up in the air and clicking her heels together with excitement. Her eyes glistened and her mouth watered at the sight of all the fat, juicy berries all around her; and she wished she hadn't eaten so much for lunch. Bear swaggered along with his hands clasped behind his back, as though he'd spent all his life exploring. But Ostrich was rather nervous, and kept peering over her shoulder to make sure nobody was following them. On they went through the trees, until suddenly they came to a long, straight clearing; and there they saw the long, straight lines that Owl had told them about —the lines on which the animal ran.

There seemed to be nothing to do but sit down and wait. They hadn't been waiting for long when they heard a noise in the distance. ' Choof-choo-oof-choof-choof,' said the noise. There, far off down the clearing, they saw little puffs of white smoke coming nearer and nearer. ' Jiggety-jig, jiggety-jig,' said the animal as it came running along towards them.

' Isn't it w-w-w-wonderful ? ' stuttered Bear nervously, turning to Ostrich.

But Ostrich had already buried her head deep in the sand.

' G-g-g-gorgeous,' stammered Goat unhappily from the other side of him.

Owl flew off down the clearing to meet the animal, leaving them all alone.

The animal came nearer and nearer and its noise grew louder and louder. ' Choof-choo-oof-choof-choof, choof-choo-oof-choof-choof,' it snorted.

' It d-d-d-does sound angry,' said Bear, turning to Goat.

But Goat had had enough. She tucked her head down on to her chest and put her tail between her legs and whisked off into the distance away from this new and terrifying animal as fast as her legs could carry her.

Bear decided to be brave. He whistled to cheer himself up, and stamped his feet up and down. As the animal came nearer and nearer, he got behind a tree and hoped it wouldn't see him. But it was a very thin tree, and he was a very fat bear. The animal came rattling past. Bear held his breath and shut his eyes. Suddenly something soft hit him on the end of his nose and fell to the ground. He half opened his eyes and looked down, and saw a huge sticky bun lying at his feet. He looked up; and saw a little girl leaning out of the side of the animal as it rattled away into the

distance and waving a large
red handkerchief. Bear bowed
and waved back and called
out, ' thank you for the bun.'
The animal gave a shriek, just as
Owl had said it would, and disappeared into a hole in the hillside.
Bear sat down and ate his bun.
Then he got up and tapped Ostrich.
At first Ostrich wouldn't move. So
Bear seized her neck and pulled and
pulled until her head came up out of
the sand.

' It's all over,' said Bear. ' It
isn't such a bad animal, after all.
It keeps itself to itself, and it throws
buns at you.'

' It makes a beastly noise,'
said Ostrich.

' Although my head was
deep down in the sand, its

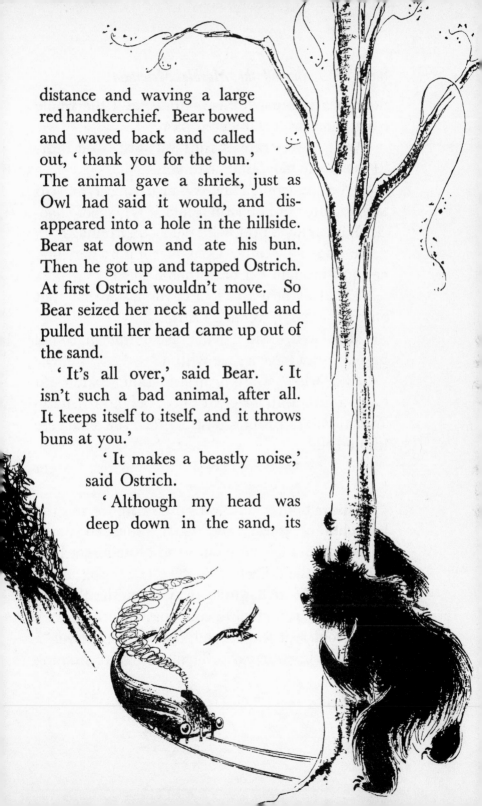

noise nearly burst my ear-drums, and the whole earth shook as it thundered past.'

' Well, at any rate, it runs jolly fast,' said Bear. ' I bet it can run faster than you.'

' I bet it can't,' said Ostrich angrily. ' No animal can run faster than me.'

' Now, now,' said Owl, ' who's quarrelling? '

He had flown after Goat to comfort her, and had just brought her back to join them.

' That silly Bear says I can't run faster than that horrible animal,' replied Ostrich.

' Very well,' said Owl. ' Next time it comes past you can have a race with it.'

' And while we're waiting,' said Bear, ' I'll build a little wall for Goat to get behind when the animal comes rushing past, so that she shan't be frightened.'

❦

So Bear built a little wall out of stones and the branches of trees; and Goat crouched down behind it and felt very safe, and quite forgot how frightened she'd been.

Owl led Ostrich a mile away down the clearing to wait for the animal to come past again.

' As soon as it reaches you, Ostrich,' said Owl, ' I shall hoot in your ear. Then you start running as fast as you can. And whichever one of you gets to Bear and Goat first will be the winner.'

Before long they heard the animal in the distance saying ' Choof-choo-oof-choof-choof.' ' Jiggety-jig, jiggety-jig,' it said as it came nearer.

Ostrich tucked her feathers into her knickers and crouched down close to the ground, with her neck stretched forward, waiting. Nearer and nearer the animal came. Its noise grew louder and louder. Suddenly Ostrich heard Owl giving a loud hoot in her ear. She gave a triumphant squawk and sprang forward and began to run like the wind, with her neck stretched forward and her eyes popping out of her head with excitement.

As soon as the animal saw Ostrich it started whistling and hooting, and hundreds of heads popped out of its side to see what was happening, including lots of little boys and girls. Everybody cheered like mad, and Ostrich squawked back at them as she ran. You never heard such a din.

' Come on, Ostrich,' yelled Bear and Goat, jumping up and down and clapping their hands with excitement.

On they came side by side. They flashed past Bear and Goat; and as the little boys and girls saw Bear they clapped their hands and threw buns at him. Bear had never seen so many buns

in all his life, and quite lost interest in the race.
But Goat came out from behind her wall and went
running after them.   Ostrich and the strange long
animal rushed away into the distance.   Ostrich
was getting very out of breath.   But she was still
just ahead of the animal.   On she rushed; and
soon she found she was going uphill.   She stopped
squawking to save her breath.   Everything suddenly seemed silent.   She looked over her shoulder.   The animal wasn't there.

' I've won!   I've won! ' gasped Ostrich, and
lay down exhausted on the grass.

Soon Owl flew up; and after him came Goat.
They had left Bear behind, blissfully happy eating
buns.

' Well done, Ostrich,' cried Owl and Goat.

' Where did the animal go to? ' asked Ostrich,
breathlessly.   ' I lost it.'

' It went into a hole in the ground,' said Goat.

' It was frightened of me! ' boasted Ostrich;
and she spread out her feathers and strutted round
and round squawking with triumph.

They stayed beside the line for many days.
Ostrich had plenty of the most exciting races.
Bear just sat beside the line all day waiting for the
animal to come past, and collected an enormous
quantity of buns.   Goat went off for long walks

every day looking for her fortune, and Owl flew with her to encourage her.

On one of her walks with Owl, Goat found a place where the animal stopped. There was a pipe sticking up by the side of the line with a thing like an elephant's trunk on the end of it. The animal had a long drink, and then said, ' Choof-choo-oof-choof-choof,' and puffed away into the distance.

' I'm sure there must be a fortune in the place that animal comes from,' said Goat. ' What a pity we can't go along with it! '

' Why shouldn't we ? ' said Owl. ' Let's collect the others.'

So they fetched Bear and Ostrich, and lay hiding near the place where the animal stopped, waiting for it to come. Just before sunset the animal came. It stopped and started drinking. They crept out of hiding. There were lots of doors in the animal's side. Bear climbed up very boldly and opened one and scrambled in. Goat and Ostrich clambered in, too, and Owl flew in after them. They shut the door quickly and looked around them. They were in a narrow room with windows at either end and lovely red bouncy seats along each side. There were pictures on the walls, and a notice on the window saying ' First Class—Smoking.' High up over the window was some poetry which said

> ' To stop the train
> Please pull the chain.'

' " Train " must be the animal's name,' said Bear, bouncing up and down on his seat.

As he spoke the train gave a shudder. A voice said 'Choof-choo-oof-choof-choof,' and they started moving. The sun set, and the lights went on in their little room, and on they went rushing through the night towards new adventures.

X

They meet a Horrible Man and run away

THE train travelled on slowly all through the night, and they kept awake in turns, in case somebody should try to get into their carriage. It ran through the forests and the fields and past sleepy little villages. When the sun rose, Owl, who was keeping watch, saw houses through the window; and then more houses; and then still more houses. The train went slower and slower. Owl woke the others up. The train gave a loud whistle and went into a black hole in the earth. When it came out on the other side they saw lots of other trains on lots of other lines, with islands between the lines and lots of people standing on the islands. The train slowed down and then stopped.

Bear stood gazing stupidly out of the window. ' So that's what Man looks like! ' he muttered to himself. ' How silly! '

Ostrich was moaning sadly in a corner. ' I'm sure somebody will want to come into our room,' she was saying. ' Then they'll take all my

feathers off for their women to put in their silly
hats and they'll put me in the Zoo.'

' Get down and hide, sillies,' hissed Owl
savagely. ' And you, Bear, hold on to the door
and stop anybody getting in.'

So they all lay on the floor. And Bear took
hold of the strap on the window and held on
tight.

' Here's an empty carriage,' they heard somebody saying outside.

The handle of the door turned. Somebody
outside pulled the door, and Bear pulled back,
holding on to the strap and grunting quietly.

' Oh dear! the door's stuck! ' the person outside
said; and they heard him walking away.

Bear went on tugging away at the strap. One
or two more people tried the door; but Bear held
on tight. At last somebody walked past the
window waving a green flag and blowing a
whistle. The train said ' Choof-choo-oof-choof-
choof' and started moving. It went faster and
faster, and soon they were away from all the
houses and out in the fields again.

They stopped at two or three more places. But
each time Bear held on to the strap on the door so
that nobody could get in; and they all kept out of
sight. Late in the afternoon they saw something

out of the window that made them grunt and bleat and squawk with excitement. Water! Absolutely nothing but water for miles and miles and miles; bouncing up and down and making funny little white splashes as it bounced, with the sky sitting on top of it in the distance.

' That's the sea,' said Owl, who knew practically everything.

' What a perfectly lovely place! ' exclaimed Goat. ' I'm sure I could find my fortune here. What a pity the train doesn't stop so that we could all get out! '

Bear looked at the piece of poetry over the door.

> ' To stop the train
> Please pull the chain '

he read out.

' Alas,' said Ostrich. ' You have to pay five pounds if you pull it. And none of us has any money at all. Not even a single penny.'

' What is money? ' asked Bear, who had never been to school and really didn't know.

' Money is what Man uses,' said Owl, ' when he wants something he hasn't got. He finds somebody who has got it, and gives him money and takes the thing away.'

' How stupid Man is! ' said Bear. ' If I see

somebody with a thing I want, I just go up and take it. I don't see the use of money. I shall pull the chain, and if any Man comes along and asks me for money I shall growl at him and tell him to go away.'

' You mustn't, you mustn't,' squawked Ostrich. ' If Man sees us, he'll catch us and put us in the Zoo. Man is terribly, terribly clever. We won't stand a chance.'

While they were arguing, the train slowed down suddenly and stopped. They threw themselves down on the floor to keep out of sight, and Bear held on tight to the strap to stop anybody getting in. They heard people running up and down the platform and doors slamming. One or two people gave a pull at the door and then passed on. The train said ' Choof-choo-oof-choof-choof ' and started moving; and Bear let go of the strap. He was too soon. There was a running noise outside. The door was flung open. And a Man burst into the carriage, slammed the door behind him, and sat down.

❧

' Phew! ' said the Man, gasping. He looked round him and saw a Bear, a Goat, an Owl and an Ostrich in the carriage with him. ' Phew! ' said the Man again : and ' Golly! '

'I hope you don't mind travelling with us,' said Goat nervously.

The Man said nothing; but his face went white, and he just stared and stared and stared.

'I've seen this Man somewhere before,' said Bear. 'I think he looks horrid.'

'There was a picture of him on the mantelpiece when I first came to stay at Mappin Villa,' said Owl. 'I thought it was so ugly that I took it

away with me one morning and dropped it in the river.'

Ostrich suddenly rose from her corner and advanced on the Man with her feathers flapping angrily. She stood over him glaring. ' Are you Mr Murgatroyd? ' she demanded.

' I am. I am,' gasped the Man.

' This,' said Ostrich, turning to the others, ' is the Man who was unkind to animals. This is the Man whose house the kind monkeys took away so that we could live in it. What shall we do with him? '

They gathered round him, and the wretched Mr Murgatroyd gasped and trembled.

' Well,' said Bear, after a bit; ' after all, we have got his house. I think if we just tease him, that will be enough.'

So Bear gave him a playful hug. And Owl flew down and pulled his tie out and pecked all the buttons off his clothes. They made him stand up, and Goat butted him two or three times. They made him lie down, and Ostrich tickled him all over with her feathers till he screamed for mercy. Then Bear sat on him for a bit to keep him quiet, while Owl read him a very long lecture and made him promise never to be unkind to animals again.

' But he'll never be any good until he gets a new face,' said Bear.

After a bit they decided they'd teased Mr Murgatroyd enough and let him go. Goat, who was very kind-hearted, even gave him some of her milk to drink. But he couldn't be trusted. Suddenly, when they weren't looking, he jumped up on to the seat and pulled the chain. There was a screech and the train stopped.

' Quick ! ' yelled Owl. ' Open the door and jump out and run ! '

Bear didn't wait to turn the handle. He hurled himself against the door, and it broke and he fell out on to the line. Goat and Ostrich jumped out of the carriage on top of him. The line was running along an embankment, and they rolled over and over down its side. When they came to the bottom they picked themselves up and ran into the trees, and went on running and running and running away from the train as far and as fast as they could go. Suddenly they came to the end of the trees. In front of them was some lovely golden sand, and beyond that for miles and miles and miles stretched the sea.

Back at the train everybody was gathering round Mr Murgatroyd. When he tried to tell them all about Bear, Goat and Ostrich, nobody would believe him. They made him pay five pounds for pulling the chain, and two pounds for a new door for the carriage, and thirty shillings for mending all the springs in the seat that Bear had broken by bouncing up and down.

Meanwhile the sun was setting, and Bear, Goat and Ostrich were very tired. They dug a great big hole in the sand, and lay in it and covered themselves up until only their heads were showing, and went off to sleep. Then Owl flew off and perched on the topmost branch of a very high tree; and stood there looking out dreamily as the moon rose higher and higher over the silvery sea.

XI

They go to Sea in a Boat

THEY slept on in the warm sand for hours and hours. Then, just before the sun rose up out of the sea, as Bear was snoring away happily and dreaming a lovely dream, something splashed him in the face.

' Stop it, Goat,' he grunted angrily.

Ostrich was splashed at the same time. ' Don't play the giddy goat,' she squawked.

' It wasn't me,' protested Goat. ' Somebody splashed me, too.'

' Well, whoever did it, please don't do it again,' growled Bear.

They turned over on their sides, and were just about to go to sleep again when there was a terrific splash and water poured all over them.

' Help, help! ' spluttered Bear; and Goat bleated with terror.

The water went away; and, raising their heads, they looked and saw that the sea had come right up to them in the night. They struggled out of their hole in the sands, and stood around unhappily

shaking the water off their bodies.   Suddenly the
sea came rushing at them again, and they turned
and ran for dear life.

Owl had heard them grunting and bleating and
squawking, and flew down anxiously to meet
them.   He heard their story.

'Oh dear; that's the tide,' he said; and explained how every day the sea goes away and
comes back and then goes away again.

'Why didn't you tell us about it last night, you
stupid bird,' growled Bear, 'instead of leaving us
there to get wet?'

Owl was very apologetic.   'You run round on
the sands and get dry,' he said, 'and I'll get some
sticks and make a lovely big fire for you to get
warm by and cook the breakfast.'

The sun had just got up out of the sea.   Ostrich
was very afraid somebody would see them; so
she buried her head in the sand to hide.   Bear
and Goat had a lovely game of leap-frog over her
back, and soon got dry again.   Then Owl hooted
to them, and they gathered round the fire and
had an enormous breakfast of eggs and milk and
honey.

The sun shone all through the next five days.
And the moon shone all through the next five

nights. Bear, Goat and Ostrich had a terrific time. Bear built the most tremendous sand castles, six feet high and more, with wonderful tunnels through them and moats all round them. He never seemed to tire of digging. Goat fetched water, in a bucket they had found on the beach, to fill up the moat, and went around collecting coloured shells and different sorts of seaweed to decorate Bear's castles. Ostrich ran enormous races with herself up and down the sands, and practised jumping over Bear's castles. Owl just sat in the sun all day warming himself and thinking how nice it was to be at the seaside. There were some lovely rocks to climb on; and some lovely pools to paddle in. Ostrich, with her feathers tucked into her knickers, used to go paddling out to sea on her long, thin legs. She went quite a long way out one day, until a big wave came and broke right over her head, and she splashed back to shore, squawking with rage. At low tide they went down to the sea to catch shrimps in the pools for supper. And after supper they lay down on the sand, higher than the tide ever came; and Owl told them wonderful stories about boys and girls until they went off to sleep.

Goat was so happy playing about on the sand that Owl began to hope she had forgotten all about seeking her fortune. But one day the three animals were playing leap-frog. They went on leap-frogging and leap-frogging for a long, long way—much farther than they'd ever been before. And suddenly they came to a boat. They went up to it cautiously, in case anybody should see them. But nobody was about. And there it was : a simply lovely brown boat with green seats in it. And on the side, painted in large gold letters, was the name FORTUNE HUNTER.

Goat went very white, and waggled her beard gravely. ' We must leave this happy place,' she said. ' I must take this boat and go off to seek my fortune.'

They were all very sad at first. But Bear soon decided it was going to be rather fun going to sea in a boat. So they yelled for Owl. They kept on yelling for two minutes, and nothing happened.

' What a tiresome bird ! ' said Bear. ' I expect he's fallen asleep. Now we'll have to go all the way back and fetch him.'

So they leap-frogged all the way back along the sands. And, sure enough, there they found Owl fast asleep, and snoring very loudly. They shook him and woke him up, and told him how they had found the FORTUNE HUNTER. Owl thought it

would be lovely to go to sea. So they all started packing and getting ready to go off.

Bear packed lots of gorgeous shells that he had found on the rocks; and Goat packed some pieces of seaweed that popped when the weather was going to be fine. Ostrich insisted on taking a bucketful of shrimps.

Then they just danced their way over the sands and down to the boat. Ostrich and Goat clambered in and Owl flew round and round overhead telling them what to do. Then Bear pushed the boat into the water and as soon as it was launched, jumped in, nearly sinking it with his weight as he did so. Goat pulled away at the oars and soon Bear took another pair of oars and helped her. They went over the sea at a fine speed and soon they were well away and out of sight of land.

&

Goat was very excited to find a fishing-rod and line in the bottom of the boat. She soon stopped rowing; and, as Bear took them out to sea, Goat fished, and soon had a lot of lovely fish for them to eat for supper. Owl flew round and round over the boat, looking out for land. He was hungry for worms. But there was no land to be seen. Nothing but the calm blue sea all around them.

They rowed on for four hours. As the sun got lower, they stopped rowing and had some supper. The fish were good to eat. They threw them up in the air and caught them in their mouths. Bear jumped about so much that they had to tell him to stop in case he turned the boat over. Goat's milk had never tasted so sweet. Ostrich gave them some lovely eggs. They didn't dare to light a fire in the boat to cook them, as Mrs Beeton would have done. So they had to teach Goat to suck eggs—a thing her grandmother had never taught her. After the sun set it got very cold out on the open sea. They all huddled close together in the bottom of the boat for warmth; and went to sleep.

A wind sprang up in the night and the sea got very rough. The boat bobbed up and down like a cork and the big waves broke over it. Bear, Goat and Ostrich felt very sick and got very wet and cold. They were glad when the night ended and the sun rose. Goat and Ostrich sat up in the boat and started getting breakfast ready. Bear was feeling very sick and grumpy, and wouldn't move. He had been bumped about a lot in the night and had a very sore head. Whenever they went near him he growled.

Suddenly they heard a loud hoot overhead,

and the sound of an excited bird flapping its
wings.

' Land ahead! Land ahead! ' yelled Owl.

They all stood up to look.   Even Bear stood up.
And there, sure enough, in the distance, near the
rising sun, was land rising up out of the sea.
They could see it quite clearly when the boat rose
up on top of a wave—a rocky, craggy piece of land,
with three trees on top of it.   When the boat sank
to the bottom of the wave they lost sight of it.
But when they rose up on the next wave, there it
was again.

' It must be an island,' squawked Ostrich,
flapping her feathers with excitement.

' It is! It is! ' bleated Goat.   ' It must be my
Fortune Island.   Quick, beautiful Bear, take up
your oars and ROW.'

They looked around them hurriedly.   Where
were the oars?   They were nowhere to be seen.
And with a big thing like an oar in a small thing
like a boat, there aren't many places to look.   The
oars were lost.

' Oh dear! oh dear! ' sobbed Goat.   ' A wave
must have come and washed them away in the
night.   Whatever shall we do! '

' We shall swim,' said Bear.

It was true that none of them except Bear knew

how to swim. But Bear always liked to try to be
helpful if he could.

It was very lucky for them that Owl had been to
school and knew everything. The wind was
blowing towards the island.

'Stand up in front of the boat, Ostrich,'
ordered Owl. 'Face the island and spread your
wings out over your head.'

Ostrich did as she was told. And Bear and
Goat crouched down and held on to her legs, in
case the wind should blow her out of the boat.
Her wings made a lovely sail. And, with the
wind behind them, they drifted slowly towards
the island. It was very cold for Ostrich; but she
held on bravely.

The closer they came to the island, the more
beautiful it looked. Lovely sands, and rocks on
the shore. Green hills beyond. Lovely bushes
covered with berries. Lovely trees covered with
coco-nuts and dates. And enormous craggy
mountains beyond the hills, for Goat to go
climbing on.

The wind blew their boat right up on to the
shore. They jumped out, and pulled the boat
right away up the beach, in case the tide should
come and take it away from them. Then they
joined hands and danced round together on the

sands, singing. Owl flew away for a bit to explore. Soon he came back, very excited.

'Come and see what I've found,' he hooted.

They followed him a little way across the sands until they came to a large Notice-Board.

'Oo-oo!' they all cried, Goat loudest of all.

For on the Notice-Board, written in large golden letters, were the two words ' FORTUNE ISLAND '.

XII

Goat finds the Treasure

GOAT and Ostrich danced up and down with excitement, and Goat started turning somersaults over and over on the sands. Bear's head was still very sore after the rough night in the open boat; and he found Goat's bleating and Ostrich's squawking rather trying. So he walked away across the sands and sat down on an oak chest that he found lying there. He put his sore head between his hands and listened to the plash-plash of the waves breaking on the shore.

After a bit the other animals came up to him.

'What's that box you're sitting on?' asked Goat.

'Oh, it's just an old chest I found lying here,' answered Bear.

'Do get up, dear Bear,' said Goat, 'and let's see what's in it.'

So Bear very unwillingly got up.

But when Goat opened the box and saw what was inside, he was as excited as the rest of them. The first thing they took out was an old, faded

piece of parchment.   On it was written, ' On this
island, I, Jacob Rowbotham, merchant, out of
Bristol, did deposit my Treasure in the reign of our
Good Queen Elizabeth, 1585.'

' 1585! ' said Owl.   ' What a long time ago! '

' It's the year Elephant's grandmother was
born,' said Bear, who kept a birthday book of all
the animals in the forest, and even of some of the
animals' mothers and grandmothers who didn't
live there any longer.

' Dear old Elephant,' said Ostrich.   ' I wish
he was with us now.'

The next thing Goat took out of the box were
two lovely long sharp knives studded with jewels.
He gave one to Bear and one to Ostrich, who were
simply thrilled.

' How jealous the other animals in the forest
will be of our lovely knives,' they thought;   and
then felt rather sad because none of the other
animals were there to be jealous.

Then they found a lot more knives, and put
them away in the bag as a present for the other
animals in the forest when they got back.

At the bottom of the chest was a large map.
Goat spread it out on the sands and asked Owl to
explain it to them.

The map had FORTUNE ISLAND written on it in

large letters. All round the edge was a deep, rich blue.

'That,' said Owl, 'is the sea. The yellow piece near the sea is the sand, and this green piece is the lower land and the hills. Here in the middle is a brown piece; and that is the mountain.'

'Look at that arrow up in the brown part!' said Goat excitedly. 'What is it pointing to?'

Owl came closer to the map and peered.

'The arrow points to a Cave,' said Owl, 'and in the Cave, I believe, we shall find the Treasure.'

They could hardly stop Goat from rushing up the mountain there and then. But Bear and Ostrich said they were hungry and thirsty. So Goat went off to get some berries; and Ostrich went off to find some water to drink; and Owl went off to look for worms; and Bear went off looking for bees. He hadn't had any honey for days.

They came back to the chest after ten minutes, looking very unhappy. There wasn't any fresh water anywhere on the island. There weren't any worms, and there weren't any bees. In fact, there weren't any animals or birds at all on the island. It was a very lonely place. Goat said the berries were sour and she couldn't eat them. Owl said the dates were all skin and stones, and the coco-nuts hadn't got any milk in them. However, they ate some of Ostrich's eggs and drank some of Goat's milk. Then Goat insisted on climbing up the mountain to look for the cave. Bear and Ostrich were still feeling hungry and thirsty, and said they'd go to sleep for a bit and join her later. So Goat set off up the mountain alone.

❧

When Bear and Ostrich woke up it was nearly tea-time. There was no sign of Goat. But Owl was sitting near them, reading. They called him over and decided to go walking up the hill together to look for the cave. On the way up they started talking about Mappin Villa and their old friends in the forest.

' I do miss the monkeys,' said Bear. ' They're such jolly fellows. Always up to tricks. Do you remember how they helped us to build Mappin Villa ? '

' I miss all the birds,' said Ostrich. ' This island doesn't seem natural, without any birds singing in the trees.'

' I miss my lovely bed up behind the chimney-stack on the roof at Mappin Villa,' said Owl; ' and all the lovely, fat, wriggling worms I used to go out and catch for breakfast.'

' Alas,' said Bear. ' There's nothing like your own home and your own fireplace with all your kind friends around you. I shall make a point of calling on Mrs Bee as soon as I get back.'

So they went on talking up the mountain-side until they came to the mouth of a large and gloomy cave. They stood at the entrance, not daring to go in. And as they stood there waiting they heard a very faint bleating noise. They put their ears to the ground, and heard the bleating noise clearer.

' Help! help! ' said the noise. ' I'm lost! I can't find my way out.'

It was Goat. They put their hands to their mouths and yelled out to encourage her.

' All right, Goat,' they shouted. ' We're coming! '

Bear had a large ball of string, which was lucky. He held on to one end, while Owl took the other end in his beak and flew into the cave, unwinding the string as he flew, so that he could find his way out again. There were passages in the cave which wound round and round, first right, then left; first up, and then down.

Owl flew a long way, hooting as he flew. It was a long, long time before at last he found Goat.

Goat was very frightened, and terribly glad to

see Owl again. They called out to the other animals. Then Bear tied the other end of the string to a tree outside the cave, and he and Ostrich walked through the cave, round and round and up and down, following the string, until they came to Owl and Goat. It was very, very dark, and very cold in the cave. All around they could hear water going 'drip, drip'. Now and again it dripped on Bear, and he shook himself angrily.

Goat told them she had found the Treasure. She took them on through the caves, unwinding the string as they went. After a bit they started going down and down. There was a light at the end of the passage, which grew brighter as they went on, until they came to a large cave with the daylight shining down through a shaft in the roof.

They stopped. There in front of them were ever so many great Oak Chests bound with brass. Bear walked across and opened one of them. There was a chinking sound, and a heap of gold and silver coins poured out and rolled across the floor of the cave. They opened more of the chests, and all of them were filled with gold and silver coins.

They stood there for a long time looking.

'Well, Goat,' said Bear at last, 'there's your fortune. How do you like it?'

Goat shook her head. 'Well, I think it's

lovely,' she said. 'But what am I going to do with it all?'

'I suggest that Bear should carry one of the chests out of this cave and down on to the sands,' said Owl. 'Then we can sit down and talk it all over.'

'I agree,' said Bear, as a large drop of water fell on to the end of his nose. 'Let's get out of this horrible cave as soon as we can.'

So Bear took up a chest full of coins. And they followed the string round and round through the passages until they came to the tree at the mouth of the cave, and into the fresh air again. Then they all just galloped down the mountain-side until they came to the beach. They were still very cold and shivering. So they gathered a lot of sticks and lit a huge fire to keep themselves warm.

They were silent for a very long time. And then suddenly Goat started speaking.

' I've come all this way to seek my fortune,' she said. ' Now I've found this Treasure, and I don't want it. What good is gold and silver to an animal like me? Here we are on this horrible island, where no birds or animals live; where even the berries are sour. All I want is a happy home with kind friends around me.' She started crying. ' I want to go back to Mappin Villa, and all my kind friends in the forest! '

' Hurray! hurray! So do we! ' shrieked Bear and Ostrich.

And Owl hooted with pleasure.

' You had your fortune with you all the time at Mappin Villa,' said Owl. ' There was no need to come all this way to find it.'

Then they fell to chattering about all their friends in the forest and the wonderful things they'd have to tell them when they got back home again.

' We'll start in the morning,' said Bear.

He went off for a while, and came back with four long pieces of wood; and, with his splendid new knife, started cutting away and turning them into oars. He carried on until far into the night— long after the others were asleep. And when he had finished he took the boat out and went rowing round the bay in the moonlight to try them out, humming happily to himself as he pulled away at his fine new oars.

XIII

Home Again

THEY were ready to start as soon as the sun
rose. It was a grand morning, with a wind
blowing away from the island, and white clouds
like little woolly sheep chasing each other across
the sky. Goat insisted on taking the Treasure
Chest with them. So they packed it in the bottom of the boat with the big bag and the shells and
the seaweed and all the knives and the bucketful
of shrimps and Mrs Beeton's Cookery Book.

Bear pulled away strongly at the oars, and soon
they were well away from the island and out on
the open sea. The wind was whipping up the
water; and the farther out they rowed the bigger
the waves became. They were lapping over the
sides of the boat, and Ostrich got very frightened.
She started scooping the water out of the boat with
her wings. But still the waves kept breaking in
over the sides.

' The boat's too low in the water,' said Owl.
' We shall have to throw something overboard.'

They looked at each other. There was only

one thing to throw : the Treasure Chest. With
all the gold and silver coins in it, it was terribly
heavy. Goat was very upset. But at that
moment an extra big wave splashed over them and
filled the bottom of the boat with water. It was
enough. They scooped out a little pile of coins,
enough to give one to each of the animals in the
forest. And then Bear seized the Treasure Chest
and heaved it over the side. There was a terrific
splash as it sank out of sight; and Bear nearly
fell out of the boat as it rocked to and fro. But
the boat was much lighter. And, as Bear took up
the oars and pulled away again, it skimmed over
the water at a fine speed and the waves stopped
breaking into it.

‘ I’m glad we’ve got rid of all that gold and
silver,’ said Ostrich. ‘ It kept reminding me of
that beastly cave on that horrible island. And
anyway we didn’t want the silly stuff.’

Bear was pleased, too. ‘ It’s the sort of stuff
people like Mr Murgatroyd would do anything
to get,’ he said. ‘ But give me plenty of honey
and a nice warm bed and you can keep all your
gold and silver.’

Goat waggled her beard gravely. ‘ I expect
I’ll get used to it,’ she said. ‘ But it does seem
a pity coming all this long way and finding all

that gold and silver, and bringing so little of it back with us.'

She picked up the rod and line and started fishing, so that they could all have a treat for their lunch.

As Bear went on rowing away into the morning, Owl flew up high in the air to see where they were going. Then he flew away out of sight, and after a bit he came back with hundreds of seagulls. The seagulls flew round and round the boat crying out, ' Walk, walk, walk.'

Ostrich was delighted to see so many birds again; but Bear was angry at first.

' What's the good of saying " Walk, walk, walk ", when we've only got the sea to walk on,' he grunted.

However, when Owl explained how the seagulls were going to help them, they all broke into cheers. The seagulls were going to lead them to the coast where the great river which flowed down from the Marble Mountain and through their very own forest came out to the sea. All day long the seagulls flew in front of the boat crying out, ' Walk, walk, walk.' And in the evening they came in sight of land.

There ahead of them was a big harbour, with lots of little ships afloat in it. As the sun set,

the lights went on at their masts, and in the
windows of the town around the harbour. They
waited until it was quite dark, and then rowed
into the harbour amongst the shipping. Goat
and Ostrich lay down in the bottom of the boat
and hid in case anybody should see them. Bear
crouched down and pulled away at the oars, so
that anybody seeing him would have thought he
was a fat old fisherman rowing home to his supper.
The seagulls flew on ahead to show them the way,
and soon they were safely through the town and
rowing up the deep, broad river through the
countryside behind it.

At first the countryside was flat. They passed
under a lot of bridges. And near one of these
bridges they heard a noise in the distance saying
' Choof-choo-oof-choof-choof '. The noise came
nearer and nearer, and a train rattled over their
heads as they rowed under the bridge. But
nobody saw them or threw any buns out of the
window for Bear.

Soon they came to some hills, and then to some
trees. The river wound in a great bend round
a tall mountain. Still Bear went on rowing
through the night. They were so longing to get
back to all their friends in the forest! Now and
again Goat took a turn at the other pair of oars.

But Bear went on rowing away all the time. It was still dark when they came to the town at the edge of their own forest. They rowed on boldly right into the middle of the town, until they came to the great white bridge over the river. Bear rowed into the bank, and they jumped out of the boat and ran up the slope into the streets of the sleeping town.

Then they ran. Bear had never run so fast in his life. All through the streets of the town they ran, not caring how much noise they made. Goat was bleating, and Ostrich was squawking with excitement, and Bear gave great deep happy grunts as he thudded along on the cobblestones. They ran through the town and up the hill and through the fields beyond. And just as the sun rose they came to the edge of the forest.

🜚

They stopped for a bit on the edge of the forest to get their breath back. The sky had never looked so blue or the fields so green. The trees of the forest beckoned to them as they swayed in the morning breeze. Bear, Goat and Ostrich looked at each other; and their eyes were bright and happy. They were laughing with joy to be coming home again, and all the world seemed to be laughing with them.

Bear looked around them. 'Where's Owl?' he said.

Owl was nowhere to be seen. They called out to him to come and share their happiness. And as they called out a voice from the trees above them called out, 'Tu-whu. Tu-whit, tu-whu.' And there was Owl calling to them to follow him. They walked into the forest.

Suddenly there was a buzzing noise, and Mrs Bee with all her court came buzzing through the trees to meet them. Bear was overjoyed to see her. Then there was a chattering noise, as hundreds of monkeys came swinging towards them from branch to branch across the tree tops crying out, 'Welcome home'. The birds were all singing out to greet them. The insects chirped away merrily. The animals came out in their hundreds to cheer Bear, Goat and Ostrich on their way. There had never been anything like it in the forest before. Owl had flown on ahead to spread the news; and everything that lived in the forest had come out to greet them.

They gave a lovely shiny coin to each of the birds and animals; gold for the girls and silver for the boys. Bear gave one of the splendid knives he had found to each of the monkeys, because he was so fond of them. Goat gave some shells to each of the other animals; and when they put their ears to them, they could hear the waves breaking on the beach.

Ostrich gave the shrimps out of her bucket to her friends the birds. But Goat kept the seaweed to hang outside the door at Mappin Villa, so that they would always know when it was going to rain.

There was a heavy thud of large feet, and suddenly kind old Elephant came into sight, swinging his trunk to and fro and honking out his welcome. ' You must be very tired,' he honked. ' Climb up on to my back, and I'll give you a ride back to Mappin Villa.'

So up they climbed. Goat in front; Bear in the middle; and Ostrich hanging on behind. Then Owl flew down and perched on kind Elephant's big, broad head. And Elephant waved his trunk in the air and started off. First he started walking. Then he started trotting. Then he started running. And Bear, Goat and Ostrich bumped up and down on his big, broad back. They went along at a grand speed, past all the cheering animals; and soon they came into the clearing.

There was Mappin Villa, just as they had left it. Bear's huge bell was standing outside the

door. The hedge they had built for Goat was
covered with huge ripe berries. The smoke was
curling up lazily from the chimney. Bear, Goat,
and Ostrich slid down off Elephant's back and
thanked him for giving them such a lovely ride.

'Not at all,' he said, bowing politely. 'I
can't tell you how happy all the animals in the
forest are to see you home again.'

They opened the front door and walked in.
There was an enormous hot breakfast waiting for
them. They sat down and ate and ate and ate.

'What I like about home,' said Bear, after they
had finished, 'is the gorgeous food you get
there.'

He folded his arms on his furry chest and went
off to sleep.

'What I like about home,' said Ostrich yawning
'is my nice comfortable bed.'

She went upstairs, and soon was fast asleep and
dreaming.

'What I like about home,' said Goat, 'is that
everybody's so kind. This is my Fortune, and
here I'm going to stay.'

She thought she ought to make a speech, and
stood up on her hind legs, but everybody had
fallen asleep. So she went upstairs, too; and
with her beard waggling up and down outside the

sheets as she breathed she went off into the land of dreams.

Owl smiled happily. He flew out of the window and told the birds and the animals who were gathered in the clearing to keep quiet so as not to disturb Bear, Goat and Ostrich. Then he flew up to his bed behind the chimney-stack and went into a happy sleep, while the sun shone down on him out of the deep blue sky.

PART II
Back to the Marble Mountain

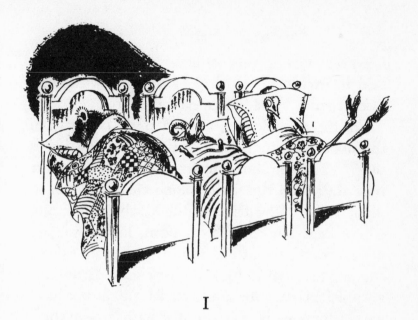

I

They wake up and hear all the News of the Forest

BEAR, Goat and Ostrich were fast asleep in the big front bedroom in Mappin Villa. Owl was fast asleep, too, in his cosy corner on the roof behind the chimney-stack. They had just come back to their home in the forest after a very long journey together. All they wanted to do was to sleep; and to go on sleeping for days and days.

It can be very noisy in the forest, especially when all the animals are talking at once. And when all the birds start singing, too, you can hardly hear yourself think. Near Mappin Villa, however, it was very quiet. ' Sh! ' the animals said to each other as they passed down the long forest road. ' Sh! ' whispered the birds.

For three whole days all that could be heard in the house was the sound of Bear grunting in his sleep. The sun shone down all day out of a clear blue sky; and the moon shone clear and full at night. Far in the distance, the Marble Mountain, where Bear and Goat were born, looked silently out across the Great Plain towards the forest. All the world seemed to be asleep and dreaming; and Bear, Goat, Owl and Ostrich might not have woken for a week or more if it hadn't been for a peculiar accident which happened to Owl.

Early one morning, Owl was having a glorious dream about worms. Most of the worms were fat and easy to catch. That was how Owl liked them. But one of the worms in his dream was rather a cheeky worm that kept wriggling out of the way every time he flew down to peck it. Owl was cross. He gave an angry flap of his wings. It was a terrific flap; and it knocked the pot right off the chimney-stack.

The chimney-pot rolled down the roof, saying ' Blipperty-blop! Blipperty-blop! ' as it went. It bounced off the edge and flew through the air saying ' Wheesht! ' as it fell. It hit the ground just near the sundial and said 'Smash!' as it broke into hundreds of little pieces.

Bear, Goat and Ostrich woke up with a start, one after the other.

'Who's that saying " Blipperty-blop " ? ' growled Bear.

'Stop saying " Wheesht ",' muttered Goat.

'Something's broken,' said Ostrich.

As they yawned and rubbed the dust out of their eyes, Owl flew in through the bedroom window, to say how sorry he was. But Bear looked so angry at having been woken up that Owl flew out again almost at once. He didn't go back to the roof, however, but flew into the house through one of the downstairs windows, which somebody had left open, and went into the kitchen.

Bear, Goat and Ostrich had a drowsy talk for a little while about nothing in particular. Ostrich wanted to know whether it was Wednesday morning or the middle of next week. She knew they had been asleep for a long, long time. Goat thought they might perhaps go to bed again, if only Owl would promise to stop rolling chimney-pots down the roof. Bear knew there was something he wanted very badly, and couldn't quite think what it was. Suddenly a lovely frying smell came floating up the stairs. Then they knew just what they were waiting for; and they all went tumbling downstairs to eat the breakfast which kind Owl was getting ready for them.

It was a marvellous breakfast, with everything they liked best. All the animals of the forest had crept into the house while they were asleep, bringing them something special to eat when they woke up. There was honey from the bees, nuts from the monkeys, fish from the beavers, lots and lots of fruit and frogs, a basinful of worms and a great pile of ripe, juicy berries specially picked for Goat.

Bear soon forgot how cross he'd been with Owl. It's always a mistake to quarrel with the cook, anyway. He could only think how kind and friendly everybody was. All the same, when he heard a knock on the door, he felt much too full to get up and answer it. Ostrich went and opened the door; and there was a secretary bird with a large, jolly-looking letter. Ostrich asked him in, and Goat took the letter and opened it, using her horns as a paper-knife.

Goat bleated with excitement. ' It's an invitation from the monkeys,' she cried. ' They're giving a party.'

' Goody! Goody! ' cried Ostrich. ' I hope they have some races, and lots of prizes for the creatures who win them.'

Bear gave a happy grunt. ' There's always lots of good food at a party,' he said; ' and plenty of fun.' He was very fond of the monkeys, and shut his eyes and thought what a lovely time he was going to have.

' Well,' said Owl to the secretary bird, ' it is nice to see you again after all this time. I hope you'll stay and eat a few worms with me and tell us what's been happening in the forest.'

' I fear,' said the secretary bird, ' that I was just flying off to see some friends of mine. However, I can spare you a few minutes.'

He settled down on the table and helped himself to a worm.

' The most important thing I have to tell you about,' said the secretary bird, ' is the Rules. My friends and I find that some of the creatures in the forest are getting very rude and tiresome. So we secretary birds have made some Rules to tell everybody what he mustn't do and when he mustn't do it; and we've put a copy of the Rules on all the most important trees in the forest.'

' What happens if the animals can't read? ' asked Bear, who was always very practical.

' Oh dear! I hadn't thought of that,' answered the secretary bird, sadly.

' Tell us some of these Rules,' said Ostrich, hiding a yawn.

' No animal,' recited the secretary bird, ' shall pull another animal's tail. No creature,' he continued, ' shall bark, grunt, howl, hoot, roar or hiss when another creature is trying to go to sleep. No bird shall be allowed to catch worms until an hour before sunrise. It was getting quite intolerable,' added the secretary bird. ' I and my friends wake up at a sensible time, and some terrible early birds were catching all the best worms and leaving none for us.'

He helped himself to another worm. ' These are delicious,' he said, looking at Owl suspiciously.

' Somebody must have got up very early indeed to get them.'

' They sound most valuable Rules,' said Owl, changing the subject hastily. ' I should like to add a Rule that bears must always be polite to birds, and that ostriches must never be late for meals.'

' I should like a Rule that everybody must plant a hedge,' said Goat, ' and that only goats shall be allowed to eat it.'

' I,' said Ostrich, sadly, ' should like a Rule that nobody must tease ostriches, or make jokes about their long necks.'

' The only Rule I want,' said Bear, ' is one that bears shall be allowed to do just as they like. I haven't much use for Rules anyway. Tell me,' he went on; ' do you think the animals will take any notice of these Rules ? '

' Most of them will, I hope,' said the secretary bird; ' but I haven't much hope of the monkeys. When we told them about the Rules, they turned head over heels and laughed. And there's a Rule that everybody must be kind to secretary birds, but I'm afraid nobody will take that very seriously.

' To proceed with my story,' went on the secretary bird, ' we have dealt while you were asleep with a very irritating woman. What a tiresome woman she was indeed! We found her wandering about on the edge of the forest calling out "Nanny! Nanny! Nanny!" in a silly, squeaky voice, until none of the animals could get to sleep and all the birds stopped singing.'

'I once knew a simply dreadful woman, who was very cruel to me!' said Goat with a shudder. 'They called her "Crosspatch". It was long, long ago, before I came to live at Mappin Villa. She used to tie me up in a field and milk me. Oh, dear! Oh, dear! I hope she isn't looking for me.'

Goat looked really frightened.

'Miss Crosspatch was the woman's name,' said the secretary bird; 'but I don't think she'll ever trouble you again. At first we tried to frighten her. The monkeys hid behind the trees and threw coco-nuts at her; but she only picked them up and threw them back. The birds and the animals made the most terrifying noises at her; but I think she must have been deaf. Then yesterday one of the birds flew after her and found out where she lived on the other side of the Marble Mountain.

'As soon as the sun set, hundreds of monkeys went out and took her house down, brick by brick, without waking her up. They left her sleeping all alone in a cold, open field. It was such a busy night! They brought the house back all the way across the Great Plain and built it up again in the forest before the sun rose. I don't expect we shall ever see or hear of that horrid woman again.'

They were all thrilled at the news. Animals like forests and so do birds, who are very fond of trees. But on a stormy night, when the wind is whistling through the branches and everyone is looking for shelter, a house is very warm and comfortable. How lucky we are, they thought, to live in Mappin Villa. And now the clever monkeys had built another house in the forest, with beds to sleep in and plenty of food in the larder, and smoke curling up to the sky out of the chimney pot.

' Who is going to live in it? ' asked Owl.

' The monkeys themselves,' replied the secretary bird. ' They call it Crosspatch Cottage. You never saw such a jolly place. It's full of monkeys right up to the roof, and it will be open to all their friends from morning till night.'

' Is that where the party's going to be? ' asked Goat.

' Yes,' answered the secretary bird. ' It's going to be a real celebration. There are going to be lots of secrets and surprises. I can't tell you any more. It would spoil all the fun.'

He took a dandelion clock from the bowl of flowers on the table and puffed at it several times. ' Goodness gracious me! ' he exclaimed. ' I hadn't realized how late it was getting.'

He bowed to them all politely, and flew away out of the window with a fat, wriggling worm in his beak.

II

The Monkeys' Party

BEAR, Goat, Owl and Ostrich arrived at Crosspatch Cottage in very good time for the
monkeys' party. It was a jolly house, just as the
secretary bird had said, with a mat outside saying
' WELCOME ' and a big brass knocker on a green
front door. Bear stepped up and knocked, and
the knocker said, ' Rat-a-tat-tat,' in the most
friendly way.

A monkey leaned out of the window over the
porch. ' Push the door and walk straight in,' he
said.

Ostrich pushed past Bear rather rudely and
went through the door. She was soon sorry for
being rude, because a very wet sponge, which had
been balanced over the door, fell with a squelch
on her head. Bear and Goat thought this was
very funny. Ostrich wasn't so sure, but she tried
to enter into the fun of the thing, and cackled
feebly as she shook the water out of her feathers.

There was nobody in the hall when they went
in; but almost at once there was a swishing noise

and a tea-tray with three monkeys on it came sliding down the stairs. The three monkeys turned head over heels when the tray hit the bottom, and landed on their feet opposite Bear, Goat, Owl and Ostrich. They scratched their heads and bowed.

' Come into the parlour,' they said, and showed the way into a large room opening off the hall.

There was a crowd of monkeys in the room. They were standing on the mantelpiece, swinging from the lamp-holders and climbing round the picture-rails. None of them was on the floor. And they all cheered like mad to see Bear, Goat, Owl and Ostrich. ' Help yourselves to nuts,' they cried, ' and sit upon the floor.'

So Bear, who was very greedy, seized a handful of nuts, put them between his jaws and crunched. But when he bit, he found that the cheeky monkeys had taken out the kernels and had filled up the shells with ink. They had heard that Bear went blue in the face when he was angry, and they wanted to see if he went as blue as ink.

Bear spluttered angrily and then made a dart to try and grab some of the monkeys, who were chuckling at the success of their joke. He certainly was very blue in the face! But the monkeys swung up on to the picture-rail and hung there out of reach.

Then Bear picked up a handful of the nuts and started throwing them at the monkeys, who caught them and threw them back until everybody was hot and happy with the fun.

Then one of the monkeys led them off on a game of follow-my-leader. He led them into all the rooms of the cottage one after another so that they could see what a jolly place it was. They followed the monkeys as best they could; but only Owl could follow them when they climbed round the room by the picture-rail. Then the monkeys led them upstairs. ' This is the bathroom,' one of them said, and stood aside to let Goat go in first. So Goat walked in and tripped up over a piece of wire and fell head first into the bath, which was full of water.

Bear stood at the door and rocked with laughter.

He knew how annoyed he would have been if it had happened to him. But really, he thought, Goat did look very funny. Bear walked into the bathroom to get a better view, and suddenly a shower-bath over his head started spurting water all over him. He turned round, growling angrily; but saw Ostrich bubbling over with laughter. So he decided not to be cross with the monkeys.

Then the monkeys gave them some very strong trays, and they played games sliding down the stairs. Then they went into the bedrooms, and one monkey climbed on to Bear's back and another on to Ostrich's back, and they had a terrific pillow-fight, trying to knock each other off, until Bear got annoyed at being hit on the face with a pillow and snatched it and threw it away out of the window.

As they were playing, there was a knock on the door. They looked out of the window and saw that Giraffe and Elephant had arrived together. ' We won't come in,' they both cried. ' There's more room for us out in the garden.'

' Don't worry! We'll come out to you!' cried the monkeys. Some of them scrambled out of one window and jumped down on to Elephant's big, broad back; and some more scrambled out of another window and slid down Giraffe's great,

long neck. Bear, Goat and Ostrich
went downstairs and out into the
garden. But Owl flew away for
a while and perched on a
nearby tree. He was a quiet
bird, and thought the party
was getting rather rough.

Then a lot of animals
came all at once: the
badgers and the bea-
vers in one party;
Rhinoceros and
Hippopotamus
in another.
The buffaloes

came and the bisons; and even a lonely gnu and a yak. They all brought presents for the new house to make it look even jollier than it was already. The presents were all wrapped up in leaves and tied together with long grass; and the monkeys had a wonderful time undoing them.

Then some very handsome parrots came and perched in a row on the garden fence. ' Now we can have a game of musical bumps,' said Mother Monkey; ' and the parrots shall make the music for us.'

❧

So the parrots started squawking and screeching, and all the animals started jumping and jigging. They took great care not to get too close to Elephant in case the noise stopped suddenly and he sat down on top of them. Suddenly, Mother Monkey winked at the parrots and they stopped squawking and screeching and shut their beaks with a snap. All the animals sat down with an enormous bump that made the earth quake around them. The four-legged animals weren't very good at the game. They found it difficult to balance on two legs and kept on falling down before the music stopped. Soon only Bear and a few monkeys were left in.

The monkeys were so excited that they didn't just sit down when the squawking and screeching stopped. They leapt up and turned a somersault in the air; and sometimes they leapt so high that it was quite a long time before they came down again. And so it was that Bear won musical bumps; and very proud he was, too.

Then they played a game of ' touch '. Every animal who was ' He ' found it very easy to catch Rhinoceros and Hippopotamus; but none of them could catch Ostrich. So in the end, Ostrich challenged them all to try and catch her; and she ran about the clearing and dodged so fast that nobody could do it. One monkey came quite near to her one time by hiding in a tree and jumping down as she came running towards him; but Ostrich jumped right over his head and made off. In the end, all the animals joined hands and made an enormous ring round her and then slowly closed in so that she couldn't get away.

They played some more running games, and Ostrich won them all. She was a famous runner! Goat won all the jumping games, since Kangaroo wasn't there. So, to give the other animals a chance, they tied Goat on to the end of a long piece of rope. Then Goat ran round very fast in a circle at the end of the rope, and all the other animals jumped over it as she came past them. The lonely gnu did very well at that game. Nobody expected him to; but in fact he won it; and he spent most of the rest of the party asking them to play it again.

Then, as it was a very fine day, they had tea in the garden. It was a gorgeous tea and a very funny one, too. Some of the buns squeaked when you bit them. There were some things that looked like oranges; but they were full of water; and when you pressed them you could spray water all over the animal sitting opposite to you. But the most unexpected thing was when two large pink cakes started having a fight. Bear, who was just about to take one of them, nearly fell over backwards with surprise. The ' cakes ' turned out to be a hedgehog and a tortoise which the monkeys had covered all over with pink icing. There were lots of other jokes; but there were also enough real cakes and fruit to make a simply splendid tea.

While they were all busily eating, some of the monkeys crept round behind the long-tailed animals and tied their tails together. Then, when Mother Monkey appeared at the cottage door with a huge trayful of jellies, all the animals got up and ran towards her. It was comical to see

the animals with
their tails tied to-
gether, falling over
each other. It was
the greediest party the animals
had ever been to, and nobody
seemed to mind.

After tea, one of the monkeys did some wonderful juggling with ever so many coco-nuts spinning
round in the air at the same time. It made
everybody quite dizzy. Then another monkey
did some most exciting conjuring tricks. He
pulled yards and yards of pink ribbon out of
Elephant's trunk, and found a yellow jelly under
Ostrich's wing, and lots of spoons and forks hidden
under Bear's fur. Then he pulled Goat's beard
and something said ' Honk-honk '. Nobody ever
found out where the noise came from.

Then everybody started chasing everybody else. They played leap-frog and went for rides on Elephant's back and had slides down Giraffe's neck, while the bigger animals looked on. They tickled Rhinoceros and they tickled Hippopotamus; they tickled the yak and the lonely gnu, until both of them rolled over and over on their backs laughing, which they'd never been known to do before.

One of the monkeys had dressed up a Guy to look like Miss Crosspatch. They burnt it on a huge bonfire and danced round it, singing and cheering.

By then everybody was very out of breath. So they sat round in a circle, and Owl flew down from the tree and joined them when he saw that the party was quieter. They played guessing games. But none of them could guess how many monkeys lived in Crosspatch Cottage; not even Goat, who could count up to well over a hundred. Then Owl told them an adventure story, and they all sat round listening with their mouths wide open with excitement. Even the monkeys stopped chattering for a while. Then they played a simply wonderful game called Animal Grab, and after that a special forest game, called Fur and Feathers.

The sun began to set behind the Marble Mountain; and Mother Monkey called the baby monkeys indoors to bath them and put them to bed. The other animals said ' Good-bye and thank you for having me; ' and the monkeys said ' It's been a pleasure. Come again soon.' Then everybody walked or flew back to their homes in the forest.

' I've never been to such a gorgeous party,' said Bear, contentedly.

' I thought there was far too much horse-play,' said Owl, severely.

' But I don't understand what you mean,' said Ostrich, who was rather stupid. ' I didn't see any horses there. There weren't even any zebras.'

' In any case I like horse-play,' said Goat, giving Bear a push. She danced away out of reach, and Bear, Goat and Ostrich chased each other through the trees until they got back to Mappin Villa whilst Owl flew on ahead to get the supper ready.

III

Owl decides to start a School; and they write some Poetry

OWL was very upset after the monkeys' party. He flew away from Mappin Villa and spent all the night sitting on the topmost branch of a tall tree in the heart of the forest, thinking about it. When morning came, he flew off to the wood where the secretary birds lived. He was sure they would understand how he felt.

He found a number of secretary birds sitting huddled together in a circle, thinking. Now and then one of them would twitter, and the other birds would nod or shake their heads. Then there would be silence and they would all start thinking again.

' It's terrible,' said Owl, as he took his place in the circle. ' I've never met anything so rough and rude as those monkeys. They show no respect at all for a wise old bird like me. And they ignore every one of the Rules clever birds like you make. They pull the tails of other animals, and even tie them together in knots. They hide in

the trees and throw coco-nuts and other things at
the passers-by; and they play the naughtiest jokes
and tricks on the most innocent creatures. The
other animals think it's funny and are getting
naughty and cheeky, too. Only the other day
Elephant blew water all over me from his trunk,
a thing he would never have thought of doing if
the monkeys hadn't put him up to it.'

' I agree that it's getting very serious,' said the
Chief Secretary Bird. ' We shall have to put a
stop to it.'

They talked for a long time. Some of them
wanted to make a prison for the naughty creatures,
but they agreed that would be no good because
the monkeys would only climb over the walls and
get away.

' The trouble,' said one secretary bird, ' is that
they don't know any better.'

' We shall have to teach them,' said a second.

' Why not start a school, then?' said a third.

' Splendid!' they all cried together. ' We shall
have a school, and Owl shall be the Head Master.'

Owl was very flattered. He thought it was a
splendid idea. He arranged for some of the
secretary birds to help him with the teaching; and
other secretary birds arranged to bring the birds
and animals along to the school so that Owl could

teach them. They decided not to let the other birds and animals know why they were starting the school, but just to make it sound as though it was going to be a lot of fun for everybody.

When Owl got back to Mappin Villa, Bear, Goat and Ostrich all asked him where he'd been. When he told them about the school, they were simply thrilled and offered to help with the teaching.

Owl looked at them sadly. ' I'm afraid you'll have to come and learn with the other animals,' he said.

' But I can read,' protested Bear.

' Yes, but you write very badly, and you can't spell, and you aren't any good at sums,' answered Owl.

' I can count up to one hundred and twenty-three,' protested Goat.

' When you come to my school,' answered Owl solemnly, ' I shall teach you to count up to one hundred and twenty-four.'

' I shall take the singing class,' announced Ostrich.

They all laughed at that, because lots of the birds in the forest made funny noises when they sang, but none of them made quite such a funny noise as Ostrich. They decided that there was nothing that Ostrich could teach anybody except running; but Owl relented about the others, and agreed that Goat could teach the cooking, and that Bear should act as a monitor and keep the other animals in order if they talked or threw things at each other when Owl was teaching them.

❧

As they sat round the table having lunch, Owl told them he had made up a piece of poetry. They all politely asked him to tell it to them.

' A wise old Owl sat on a tree,' Owl began.

He paused and looked round at them.

Bear felt something was expected of him. ' Hey-diddle-diddle-diddle-dee,' he remarked.

' What do you mean by " hey-diddle-diddle-diddle-dee " ? ' asked Owl angrily.

' Oh, nothing much,' said Bear. ' Just " Hey-diddle-diddle-diddle-dee ".'

' But " hey-diddle-diddle-diddle-dee " isn't sense,' said Owl.

' I know it isn't,' said Bear. ' But it rhymes; and that's all that matters.'

' Does poetry have to make sense? ' asked Ostrich.

' You foolish bird,' said Owl angrily. ' I shall begin again.'

' A wise old Owl sat on a tree,' he said, and paused.

This time it was Goat who interrupted him. ' His face was as black as a cup of tea,' she said.

' But that's silly,' said Ostrich. ' Tea isn't black if you have milk in it.'

' And sugar,' said Bear, dreamily, because he was very fond of sugar.

' Sugar doesn't make any difference to the colour,' said Goat.

' No, but milk does,' said Ostrich.

' Silence, creatures,' hooted Owl angrily. ' I shall begin again. And if any of you interrupts me a third time, I shall be very cross indeed.'

So he started again.

' A wise old Owl sat on a tree.

' A picture book was on his knee . . .' he began.

' But birds don't have knees,' said Bear, before he realized what he was doing.

Owl hooted with rage. He boxed Bear's ears with a great flap of his wings, and flew out of the window to his perch up behind the chimney-stack. He was frightfully cross; and although Bear, Goat and Ostrich went out into the garden and pleaded with him to come down and finish his lovely poem, he refused to take any notice of them.

'But it was a silly poem, wasn't it,' said Bear, when they got back into the house. 'Birds don't have knees, do they, Ostrich?'

Ostrich agreed that birds didn't have knees in the same way as bears and monkeys. 'But it doesn't matter,' explained Goat. 'Poetry doesn't have to make sense so long as it rhymes.'

'Then I have made a poem,' said Bear; and he recited:

> *A Goat, an Ostrich and a Bear*
> *Said " which is what ", and " here is where ",*
> *And " who is that ", and " when is now ",*
> *And " can you kindly tell me how ? "*

'It certainly doesn't make sense,' remarked Ostrich. 'I don't understand it. Perhaps I'm not expected to.'

'It is a splendid poem,' said Goat. 'Here is one I have made up.'

> *The Owl behind the chimney-pot*
> *Knows which is which and what is what ;*
> *And once upon a time he knew*
> *Why I am I, and you are you.*

Bear and Ostrich both thought it was a fine poem. They all went out into the garden and recited their poems to Owl in the hope of cheering him up. But he pretended not to hear. So they went off for a walk together in the forest.

'Poor old Owl's getting awfully grumpy nowadays,' said Bear.

'Yes, he didn't enjoy the monkeys' party at all,' said Goat. 'And he never joins in our fun and games as he used to.'

'We must try and make his school a success,' said Bear. 'That will cheer him up.'

'I hope he doesn't teach us poetry, because I shall giggle all the time,' said Ostrich.

'And I'm afraid those naughty monkeys will tease him,' said Goat.

'We'd better go and see them and tell them they've got to be good,' said Bear.

They were always glad of an excuse to go and see the monkeys. So they made their way to Crosspatch Cottage and found the monkeys playing a most exciting game of hide and seek. They joined in the fun. And then they stayed for tea and helped to finish all the cakes and buns that were left over from the party.

The monkeys had heard all about the school, and Bear explained how he wanted them all to be very good and listen to everything that was told them so as to make Owl happy. Mother Monkey was very worried and explained that none of her children had ever been known to stay still for more than ten seconds, except when they were asleep. But Bear told her that if any monkey was naughty he would take him and throw him into the river. And he looked so fierce when he said it that all the monkeys promised to try their hardest.

After tea, Bear, Goat and Ostrich said ' goodbye ' and set off for home. On the way they called in on Mrs Bee and collected some honey. And Goat and Ostrich gathered some special worms so as to make Owl happy and let him know that they hadn't forgotten him.

When they got back to Mappin Villa, they found that kind Owl had got the supper ready. They let him have the worms, and he was very pleased and quite forgave them for being rude. He even agreed that birds didn't have knees and that his poem was rather silly. He offered to tell them another poem, and Bear and Goat sat down to listen. But Ostrich went into the garden and buried her head in the sand so that nobody would notice if she giggled.

This was Owl's poem :

'*All creatures who would like to know*
Why rivers run and forests grow,
Why water's wet and fire is hot,
And how, when, why, where, which and what ;
And where to go and what to see,
And twice times two and A, B, C,
And how to write and when to sing,
And something about everything,
Come to the School where gentle Owl,
That wise and educated fowl,
Explains it all in simple words
To insects, fishes, beasts and birds.'

'Must we have the insects?' asked Bear, scratching himself.

'I'm afraid you can't have monkeys without them,' replied Owl.

IV

A Year in the Forest

THE school was held in a clearing down by the bank of the river. The trees stood back from the river in a broad half-circle, and Owl perched on the lowest bough of a tree in the middle. He called it the Tree of Knowledge. The monkeys and the other small animals sat in the front of the class, looking up at Owl. Behind them sat the middle-sized animals. Elephant and the biggest animals sat still farther back with the river behind them. The crocodiles and the alligators and Hippopotamus and his friends swam about in the river, with their ears out of the water, listening to all that was said. The fishes floated about on the surface with their mouths wide open. A flock of secretary birds was gathered on the trees on either side of Owl to see that all the creatures behaved themselves properly.

The Chief Secretary Bird called for silence and then began to read out the Rules. ' This School shall be called Treetops College,' he said; and all the animals cheered like mad.

' All creatures,' he went on, ' shall do what they're told, speak when they're spoken to, put their paws or their wings over their mouths when they cough, and keep their eyes and ears open and their mouths shut.

' No creature,' continued the Chief Secretary Bird, ' shall pinch, kick, bite or bully another creature during school hours. All creatures shall stand up when the Head Master flies into school, and sit down again when he reaches his perch.'

He stopped and turned to Owl. And Owl began by explaining what the school was all about. He hoped that they would be good birds and animals and would learn lots and lots of useful things.

' This morning,' he said, ' we shall start off with sums.'

He looked round the class and all was silent, except for the sound of the monkeys gently scratching themselves and Elephant breathing down the neck of the animal sitting in front of him.

' If,' said Owl, ' five monkeys are as heavy as one bear, and five bears are as heavy as one elephant, how heavy are ten monkeys, eight bears and two elephants ? '

There was a pause; it was a very difficult sum; and then Ostrich held up her wing.

' Well, Ostrich,' said Owl, encouragingly.

' Please, Sir,' asked Ostrich, ' is it a riddle ? '

The other animals giggled, and Owl frowned angrily. Ostrich blushed and wished she had some sand to bury her head in.

Bear nudged the lonely gnu, who was sitting next to him. ' I know the answer,' he whispered. ' It's a catch.'

Owl overheard him. ' Well, Bear,' he said, ' what is the answer ? '

' Please, Sir,' said Bear, ' the sum's wrong. One bear weighs a lot more than five monkeys.'

' Don't be silly! ' snapped Owl. ' This is a very small bear and very big monkeys.'

'Then it must be a tiny elephant,' muttered Bear. Luckily Owl didn't hear him.

In the end the animals had to give it up. So Owl told them the answer. 'Four elephants, twenty bears or a hundred monkeys,' he said.

'Just enough for a nice game of ludo,' thought Elephant.

'What a lot of honey all those bears would want,' thought Mrs Bee.

'We should just have room for all the monkeys in Crosspatch Cottage,' thought Mother Monkey, 'if the bears and the elephants didn't want to come, too.'

Owl gave them a few more sums; but none of them seemed to be very good at sums. So they turned to spelling and got along quite well spelling each other's names until they came to Rhinoceros and Hippopotamus. Owl was horrified to find that neither of them could spell his own name. He made them come forward together and stand in front of the class and spell them out loud ten times each.

Then, when they had finished spelling for the day, Goat stepped forward nervously to give the school a lesson in cooking. She opened a book and started reading.

'Take a fish and remove its bones,' said Goat.

As soon as she had said it, everybody turned to the river and tried to seize a fish. There was a terrific splashing and plunging noise as all the fish dived down out of sight to the bed of the river. They swam away, and nobody could ever persuade them to come back to the school again.

The secretary birds called loudly for silence. But everybody was excited; and one of the naughtiest monkeys crept round behind Elephant where he sat with his back to the river. He tweaked his tail so hard that Elephant threw back his head in anger and fell over backwards into the river, right on top of Crocodile, who was swimming past when it happened.

Then there was a terrific splashing and honking and trumpeting and snapping of teeth. And Elephant struggled out of the river with his trunk full of water and sprayed it all over the monkeys where they sat in the front of the class.

Ostrich nudged Bear and reminded him of his promise to keep the monkeys in order. Bear was still annoyed about the sum which said that five monkeys were as heavy as one bear. So he strode forward and picked up five monkeys under each of his furry arms and threw all ten of them out into the middle of the river. He turned back for more and went on throwing monkeys into the river

until there weren't any of them left on the bank.
And the monkeys, finding themselves half-way
over the stream, swam across to the far bank and
made their way home across the treetops.

After that there were so few creatures left that
Owl decided to shut the school down for the day.
He was very sad at lunch at Mappin Villa, and
nothing they said or did could cheer him up.

However, all the animals turned up at school
again the next day and behaved much better.
Bear sat close to the mon-
keys, and whenever one
of them began to be rude
or cheeky, a great furry
paw would stretch out to-
wards him and he would
decide to be quiet.
The school went on
right through
the summer,

and they learnt a lot of very useful things. They were all very grateful to Owl for being so kind and patient; though everyone agreed that however long they went on going to school they would never be so wise and clever as he was.

❧

The autumn came and the leaves began to fall from the great trees of the forest. One day, all the swallows gathered together, as they did every year, and got ready to fly off towards the sunshine. All the birds and animals gathered to say good-bye to them. Ostrich gave them special messages to take to her mother in the Zoo, far, far away across the seas. And they promised to bring back news of her life in the special Ostrich house men had built so that they could bring their children to come and look at her. Then the swallows flapped their wings, and the sky became quite dark as they flew off in great flocks high up above the trees of the forest.

Winter came; and it was very cold. It had never been so cold in the forest before. Snow fell. All the little streams running through the forest froze. The animals grew thick, furry coats to keep the cold out. But it was very cold indeed for the poor birds. Bear, Goat, Owl and Ostrich kept a lovely log fire blazing away all day long in

Mappin Villa, and lots of animals and birds used to call in from the forest to warm themselves by it. The parrots were there nearly all the time, because they don't like cold weather. They always envied the swallows when they flew off to the sunshine, but were too lazy to go with them. The parrots taught Bear to say things that men and women say. He learnt to say ' Pretty Polly ' and ' Scratch my back '. And whenever he said it, Ostrich would jump with fright, because she was afraid it was a man coming to catch her and put her in the Zoo. She never quite got used to it.

When the weather was fine, they went out skating on the streams and the ponds, or toboggan-ing down the hills. Ostrich proved to be a won-derful skater. She skimmed over the ice at an enormous speed. And as she never looked where she was going, all the other animals had to keep well out of the way. One of the jolliest sights was to see Bear and Ostrich dancing together on the ice. In fact, Bear thought it all tremendous fun until one day, when he was capering about and doing a jig to show how happy he was, he broke the ice with his weight and fell through a big hole into the water. He was much more careful where he went after that, and didn't bounce nearly so much.

The monkeys weren't very good at skating. But kind Goat harnessed herself to a sledge and went skating round and round the pond pulling loads of little monkeys behind her. What the monkeys liked best was the snowballing. They threw very hard and straight; and used to hide among the branches of the trees and pelt the other animals with snowballs as they passed by.

The beavers were busy all day long building the most wonderful animals out of the snow. One day they built a really marvellous elephant with a huge icicle hanging down in front just like a trunk. It was so lifelike that Elephant, who was passing by soon after they'd finished, stopped to talk to it. He had heard of white elephants, but had never seen one before. He was rather annoyed when it didn't answer him. But then he heard all the other animals giggling and laughing around him, and when he touched it and found it was made of snow, he thought it was a splendid joke.

The winter wasn't much fun for Elephant, of course. He was too heavy to go on the ice, and his long floppy ears got very cold. The beavers did build him an enormous toboggan, and he had one ride down the hill on it. But the sight of Elephant whizzing through the air so terrified all

the smaller animals that they made him promise
never to do it again.

So the days went by, until one day the sun shone
brightly and a warm, west wind blew. The snow
melted and ran away down the hills into the
rivers; and the rivers ran bubbling and laughing
out and away towards the sea. Spring had come.
The buds were opening. The grass was bright
and green again. The birds were singing happily
on the trees. And everything in
the forest was glad and gay.

It was then that Eagle
flew down to the forest
from the crag where
he lived at the
very peak of the
Marble Moun-
tain. Eagle was
an old friend of
Bear's and had
known him
when he was a
baby. He had
a letter for him,
and another
letter for Goat.
It was from

their mothers, and told them all the news of the mountain where they had been born, and all about the friends they used to play with when they were little.

That night, after supper in Mappin Villa, Bear started talking about the big cave where he had been born near the top of the Marble Mountain. Goat, too, started talking of all the peaks and crags she used to climb, and the fine, free, happy life she used to lead when she was little. There were some extra special berries that grew in the shade beneath the ledges up on the mountain and grew nowhere else. Her mouth watered when she thought about them.

'How nice it would be to go back to the Marble Mountain,' sighed Goat, 'and to see my father and mother again, and all my brothers and sisters and cousins and uncles and aunts.'

'It would be lovely,' said Bear. 'There was some heather near the top of the mountain; and the bees who lived there made the most wonderful honey.'

'Let's go back there for a while,' said Goat. 'Come on, Bear,' she bleated eagerly; 'we'll start off to-morrow morning.'

Bear's eyes lit up with excitement, and he jumped for joy. He tried to hug Goat to show

how happy he was. But Goat danced away out of reach. She had been hugged by Bear before, and knew how much it hurt.

' Will you take me with you ? ' said Ostrich. ' It will be very lonely in the forest when you've gone away.'

' Of course you can come, Ostrich,' said Goat ; ' and you'll come along too, Owl, won't you ? '

But Owl decided he would have to stay behind to look after the school. ' I shall stay with my friends the secretary birds while you're away,' he said ; ' and I shall look in at Mappin Villa every day to make sure that everything is tidy. Perhaps on our half-term holiday at the school, I shall fly up to the Marble Mountain to see how you're all getting on.'

So Owl flew off to see the secretary birds, and they agreed that he could stay with them while the others were away. When he got back to Mappin Villa he helped them all to pack and get ready for the journey. They were all very excited. But Bear was also a little bit sad.

' I'm afraid I shall miss the monkeys while we're away,' he said.

' Then why not take one of them with us ? ' said Goat.

' You clever quadruped ! ' said Bear. ' I shall

go straight off to Crosspatch Cottage and fix it all up.'

So off he shambled through the forest. Back he came an hour later with the jolliest of all the monkeys with him, who was awfully excited to be going off with Bear, Goat and Ostrich on an expedition to the top of the Marble Mountain. Bear had found time to call on Mrs Bee on his way and had collected jars and jars of honey to take with him on the journey.

They talked for a little while; and soon Bear, Goat and Ostrich went up to bed so that they should be ready for an early start as soon as the sun rose; and Monkey went with them. But Owl flew off into the forest. There were things he wanted to do before morning: a surprise he wanted to get ready for the others to help them on their journey.

V

The Road to Ponky Poo

WHILE the others were sleeping on the night
before their journey, Owl went out and
found a useful piece of wood in the forest. He
brought it back to Mappin Villa and stayed
awake all night drawing on it a map of the
country they would be going through. It was a
wonderful map, with blue for the water and green
for the trees and yellow for the Great Plain and
brown for the mountains. He left the top of the
Marble Mountain white, because it was so very
high. He drew some very jolly pictures of the
different things that happened at the different
places on the map. Mappin Villa was in the
middle, painted in bright red, with Bear, Goat and
Ostrich leaning out of the window. In another
part of the forest, there was a picture of the
secretary birds sitting round in a circle looking
very solemn, with their beaks touching. Right
up at the top of the map was a jolly place called
Ponky Poo, the land from which elephants never
come back. Near the edge was the Marble

Mountain, with a picture of Bear's father and mother standing at the mouth of a cave and lots of goats prancing round the crags searching for berries.

Owl rather liked making things complicated. So he had called in a woodpecker; and the woodpecker had pecked away until he had turned the map into a jig-saw puzzle.

'There you are,' said Owl, when the others came down to breakfast in the morning. 'All you have to do if you get lost is to make the jig-saw puzzle and look at the map. Then you'll know just where you are.'

They gathered round and agreed that it was a fine map. They thanked Owl for being so kind and clever. Then they allowed Monkey to break up the puzzle and Bear put the pieces into a box so that they could take it with them on the journey.

Bear also gathered up his huge bell from the place where it lived outside the front door. He swung it round and round and it made such a noise that Owl had to put his wings over his ears and Ostrich buried her head in the sand until it was all over. It was so long since he had rung it to call his mother when he was lost. He swung it round and round until he was giddy and fell over on his back. He lay there happily looking

up at the blue sky. How wonderful it would be,
he thought, if he could ring the bell when they
came to the end of their journey, to let his mother
know he had come back to the Marble Mountain.

' I think I should like to go to Ponky Poo on
the way,' said Ostrich, who had been thinking
about all the places on the map. ' I used to
know an elephant who has gone to live there.
The birds bring me messages from him sometimes,
and it would be nice to see him again.'

Both Bear and Goat remembered the elephant.

' He was an awful nuisance in Mappin Villa,'
said Bear. ' Do you remember the special bed
we had to make for him? And how he was
always leaning against the walls so that we were
frightened he would knock the whole house
down ? '

' Besides, he didn't know when to go; and he
ate far too much; and he drank all the milk I
could give and still said he was thirsty,' said Goat.

' But he was very kind,' said Ostrich. ' You
can forgive an animal a lot if he's kind; even if he
does eat five of your eggs at a time. He used to
tell me he admired me. And it must be awfully
jolly at Ponky Poo with all those other elephants
there. They're so big and solid, and nobody ever
expects them to fly.'

Ostrich was very firm.   So they did the jig-saw
puzzle and looked at the long, straight road that
leads to Ponky Poo.   They decided they would
go there first as it was such a fine day and there
was plenty of time to do what they liked.   So
off they set; and Owl agreed to fly with them
for a bit to see them on the way.

Bear and Goat walked side by side with Monkey
perched up on Bear's shoulder scratching him behind the ears to keep him happy.   Bear was
carrying the luggage, including the box with the
jig-saw puzzle in it, and lots of jars of honey, and
his bell, and a large box of sand for Ostrich to bury
her head in if they couldn't find any on the way.
Ostrich walked with them for a time.   But the
sight of a long, straight road was too much for her.

' I'll run on ahead and tell them you're coming,'
she said.

So she said ' good-bye ' to Owl.   She tucked
her feathers into the knickers that she always wore
when there was running to be done.   She stretched her neck forward and ran away like the wind.
In a minute's time all they could see of her was
a small, black speck in the distance and a cloud
of dust.

' Is she mad? ' asked Monkey, who didn't
know her very well.

'Not really,' answered Bear. 'It's just a way ostriches behave, and you have to get used to it. Sometimes when you're talking to her, she'll run away in the middle of a sentence.'

'I only hope she doesn't get lost,' said Goat anxiously.

'If she does,' said Bear, 'she'll only have to hide and then we're bound to find her.'

'She certainly runs very fast,' said Monkey.

'She does indeed,' said Owl. 'But there's one race she'll never win.'

'And what is that?' asked Bear, who always wanted to know the answer to everything.

'The Human Race,' answered Owl, solemnly.

Soon it was time for school to begin, and Owl had to fly away and leave them. Bear and Goat trudged on. It was a very long, straight road indeed and looked as if it would never end. The day grew hotter and hotter as the sun rose higher in the sky. After another hour, they felt they couldn't possibly go on any longer. So they sat down under a tree and had something to eat. Bear swallowed up four great jars of honey, which he had collected from Mrs Bee the night before, and Goat went into the wood and found some berries on the bushes. Monkey scrambled up the trees and found some nuts.

Bear wanted to go to sleep, but the others wouldn't let him; so up he got and on they went. The box of sand that Bear was carrying for Ostrich seemed to get heavier and heavier; so when the others weren't looking, he put it down by the side of the path and went on without it.

The day got hotter still. Everything in the forest around them seemed to be asleep. Even the birds had stopped singing. But after a while the road got wider and wider. Then it sloped down a gentle hill and they crossed a river. They climbed up the other side, and there they found Ostrich with her head buried in a heap of sand.

They pulled her head out and she looked around her, blinking nervously. ' It's very dangerous here,' she said. ' Man has been this way.'

' How do you know ? ' asked Goat.

' I can smell him,' said Ostrich.   ' So I thought it best to hide.'

' Well, I'm very glad you did hide,' said Bear; ' otherwise we might never have found you again.'

After they had walked on together for a little way, Bear noticed something glistening in the sunlight by the side of the path.   He turned aside to see what it was.

It was a very funny thing Bear found.   Two pieces of metal shaped like a man's foot, each with four wheels on it and a strap.   Ostrich was very nervous indeed.   ' I said Man had been this way,' she said.   ' We must hide at once.'   And she ran round looking for some sand to bury her head in.

Goat wanted to hurry on.   But Bear and Monkey were interested.

' I think I see how it works,' said Bear.   ' You have to put the metal things on your feet and tie them on with the strap.'   He stooped down to try and do it.   But he was rather clumsy with his fingers; and besides, he had got very fat from eating too much honey, and it wasn't at all easy for him to touch his feet.   So he sat down, and Monkey helped him to strap the things on.

' I wonder what the wheels are for,' said Bear, standing up. Almost immediately he sat down again. This made him very cross. He stood up once more. The wheels began to turn. He rolled downhill for a few yards and then sat down again with a bump.

The others knew how much it annoyed Bear when people laughed at him, so they swallowed as much laughter as they could. But there was far too much to hold inside them, and it all came bursting out in cackles and giggles and bleats.

Bear was furiously angry. He kept on getting up and running at them and trying to grab them; and every time he tried, the wheels went round and he fell over again. He tried to pull the things off his feet; but Monkey had tied the straps on too tightly and he couldn't do it.

At last the animals couldn't go on laughing any longer. Their ribs were aching too much. Bear got calmer. He remembered how he had skated on the ice in the forest during the winter. He got to his feet and began to find it easier to move round on his wheels. As he got better and better, the others clapped him and told him how clever he was. And Bear became very pleased with himself and quite forgot how angry he had been. He found himself going faster and faster, and thought

of the day when he would be able to run races
with Ostrich and beat her.

In the end the others got tired of watching Bear
rolling around on his wheels.

' We must get on,' said Ostrich. ' Man has
been this way, and may come back again.'

But with all their running and skating they had
strayed far away from the road to Ponky Poo and
couldn't find the way back again. On the far
side of the river they could see the forest. Away in
the distance they could see the Marble Mountain.
There were no trees on their side of the river—
nothing to show them which way they should go.

' We shall have to do Owl's jig-saw puzzle and
look at the map,' said Goat.

So they took the pieces out of the box and
started fitting them together. Monkey was very
good at this. The others, particularly Ostrich,
were rather stupid, and kept on trying pieces
which couldn't possibly be expected to fit. So
they left Monkey to get on with the puzzle by
himself.

After a bit, Monkey called out, ' I've finished
it! But five pieces are missing.'

They gathered round anxiously. ' Oh, dear!
Oh, dear!' said Bear. ' That's a thing that
always happens with jig-saw puzzles.'

They searched around for the missing pieces; but there really wasn't anywhere to look. Then they came together again to look at the map. Alas! One of the pieces that was missing was the one with Ponky Poo on it. They were indeed lost!

' What a pity we haven't got Owl with us,' said Ostrich. ' He would know what to do.'

' I expect he'd fly around until he found out which way to go,' said Goat.

' It only shows how silly it is having a bird that can't fly,' said Bear, looking crossly at Ostrich.

' At any rate it's better than a Bear that loses pieces out of jig-saw puzzles,' replied Ostrich.

Bear ran at her, and Ostrich ran away. She didn't like fighting and never had any difficulty in keeping away from animals that tried to be rough. But she had forgotten about Bear's roller skates and had to run her fastest to keep away from him.

Monkey was terrified they would run out of sight and get lost. He jumped on Goat's back, seized her by the horns and urged her to run; and Goat lowered her head and galloped after Bear and Ostrich as they ran off into the distance. She wished still more that Owl was with them. He was a tiresome bird at times, but he always knew just how to stop them from quarrelling.

He would ask them a riddle, or start them playing a game. And, if they were still cross after
that, he would threaten to stop cooking for them
unless they became friends again.

Goat ran very fast; but her legs weren't long
enough, and Bear and Ostrich got farther and
farther away.

Ostrich was beginning to get quite nervous of
this terrifying new Bear on wheels. She ran faster
and faster, and still he kept close behind her,
clutching his bell as he ran. She hardly noticed
the elephant, who came galloping across her path,
until he was right on top of her.

' Where are you going ? ' she gasped.

' I'm going to Ponky Poo,' he cried. ' Sorry I
can't wait.'

Ostrich turned aside and ran after the elephant;
Bear followed; and, in the distance, Goat with
Monkey on her back followed as well. On they
went. The sun was setting behind them, beyond
the Marble Mountain. Ahead of them there were
two ranges of hills, with a narrow gap between
them. The elephant was running straight for the
gap. He went through it and disappeared out of
sight.

Ostrich came to the gap. She paused for a
moment. On either side of her were high, black

rocks. Ahead of her was the steepest, smoothest and longest slope she had ever seen, going down and down out of sight into a valley between the high, black rocks. Far below her she saw the elephant, sitting down now and whizzing away out of sight down the long, slippery slope.

Ostrich could hear Bear overtaking her on his

wheels. She didn't hesitate any longer. Over the edge she went and whizzed away down the slope faster than she'd ever been in her life before. Bear couldn't have stopped anyway. He shot over the edge and sat down and slid all helter-skelter down the slope after Ostrich. Long after that, Goat came to the slope with Monkey on her back and slid down it, bleating with excitement.

When they reached the bottom they found themselves surrounded by elephants.

' Welcome to Ponky Poo,' the elephants said.

VI

The Land of the Elephants

'WELCOME to Ponky Poo,' said the elephants again.

' I'm sorry we came in without knocking,' said Bear.

' That's all right,' said one of the elephants. ' All our visitors come in that way. Once you go over the edge you can't possibly stop until you reach the bottom.'

' And how do you ever get out again?' asked Goat.

' None of us do,' replied the elephants; ' and luckily we don't want to. It's very easy for us to come down the long, steep, slippery slope, just as you did. But no elephant could ever possibly climb up it again. You've only got to look at it and then look at us to see why.'

' That,' said another, ' is why they call this place " Ponky Poo, the land from which elephants never come back ".'

Bear began to wonder how he would ever get back himself. He decided that in any case he would have to wait until he could persuade Monkey to take the roller skates off his feet. Even without wheels, it was obviously going to be very difficult. He called for Monkey. But Monkey was already busy scratching the ears of some of the older elephants, and didn't hear him.

Meanwhile, Bear, Goat and Ostrich were very bruised after sliding down the slope, and Bear mentioned it to one of the elephants.

' That always happens to our visitors,' said the elephant. ' So we keep some special mud to heal them.'

He led them aside to a hole in the ground. There was some fine, soft, creamy mud in the hole. He spread it over their bodies and rubbed them gently with his trunk. It was very soothing indeed and made Bear, Goat and Ostrich feel very much better. Then the elephant plunged into the mud himself and wallowed about and splashed, having a wonderful time. When he came out Bear, Goat and Ostrich all thought how beautiful he looked. He seemed to have lost all his wrinkles.

' We call it a " mud bath ",' the elephant explained. ' We have a bath in the mud every day. It keeps us young and strong. You see that elephant over there,' he went on, pointing to a very large and handsome creature. 'Guess how old he is.'.

'Ten,' said Bear.

'Twenty,' said Goat.

'Thirty,' said Ostrich.

'One hundred and fifteen,' said the elephant. 'And he can still turn somersaults and pull a tree out of the ground with his trunk. He came to Ponky Poo eighty years ago and has had two mud baths a day ever since. Come over and meet him.'

So they were introduced to the aged elephant. He seemed to know all about them, and remembered their great-great-grand-parents very well. 'When I was a young elephant,' he said, ' Man hadn't come to live near the forest. We used to wander as we pleased down by the river to the sea, and had a wonderful time splashing in the waves. I'm told it has never been the same since Man came.'

'And what made you come to Ponky Poo, Sir?' asked Bear politely.

'It was Man,' answered the aged elephant. 'When he came to the land and started to build his town by the river, he took some of us elephants and made us carry things on our backs up from the sea. When he thought we weren't working

hard enough, he used to beat us with sticks. It
didn't hurt; and the weights he made us carry
weren't very heavy. But it made us sad to be
working, when we might have been playing hide-
and-seek in the forest.'

Bear decided he would like to play hide-and-
seek with an elephant. He liked winning and
thought it would be very easy. He said so, and
the aged elephant promised that they would
have a game as soon as he'd finished telling his
story.

' One day,' went on the aged elephant, ' we all
decided to run away. We didn't know where we
were going; but we thought anywhere would be
good enough so long as it was far away from Man.
So we all started running together. Man was
terrified. We roared with laughter to see him as
we all stampeded by; and that frightened him
all the more. We ran through the forest, knocking down the trees in our path as we went. We
splashed our way over the river and raced up the
hill on the other side. On we went until we came
to the edge of the slippery slope. We were all of
us going much too fast to be able to stop. So over
the edge we went, one after the other, and slid
down and down until we came to the bottom.
And here we've been ever since. Now and again

some more elephants come to join us. One of
them came this evening, just before you arrived.
We're all very happy here. None of us ever
wants to go back again. We couldn't go back
even if we wanted to, because the slope we came
down is far too steep and slippery for any of us to
climb up again; and all round the rest of the
valley are steep, high rocks which none of us could
possibly climb.'

'The more I hear about Man, the more I dis-
like him,' said Goat.

'Serve him right to have to carry his things for
himself,' said Ostrich.

'We don't think much of Man as you can

imagine,' said the aged elephant. 'That's why we call that fruit we're all so fond of " Mango ".'

'It's a wonderful story,' said Bear; 'and it's a lovely place you live in. Now can we play hide-and-seek?'

'Certainly,' said the elephant. 'Shut your eyes and count sixty and then open them and come and look for us.'

❧

So they shut their eyes, and Bear started counting. For a few seconds there was a rustling noise and after that there was silence, except for the sound of Bear counting.

'. . . . fifty-nine, SIXTY. NOW!' said Bear, opening his eyes.

He rubbed his eyes and gazed around him. There wasn't an elephant to be seen. 'Pinch me, I must be dreaming,' said Bear; and then said 'Ow!' and jumped two feet in the air. Monkey really was a wicked pincher!

Ostrich and Goat were as puzzled as he was. Ostrich was sure that if only she could find some sand, she would find all the elephants with their trunks buried in it. Goat went to see if they were hiding in the pool of mud. But there weren't any bubbles. 'They'd have to breathe if they were under the mud,' thought Goat. 'They can't possibly be there.'

They wandered down the valley searching. Monkey climbed up a tree to see if he could spy them, but they were nowhere in sight. Once they thought they heard an elephant laughing behind them, but the noise stopped suddenly as though it had stuffed its trunk into its mouth. They went on wandering around. It was ridiculous that a hundred or more huge elephants could disappear like this!

'They must be magic elephants,' said Ostrich.

In the end they gave it up and sat down to see what would happen next. Then something laughed behind them. Then something laughed in front of them. And suddenly the whole valley was full of the sound of elephants laughing. It was a noise like thunder. It echoed round and round the valley and came crashing back again from the rocks. Ostrich covered her ears with her wings to shut out the deafening noise. Bear, Goat and Monkey looked round and saw elephants all round them standing upright in the clumps of tall grass that were dotted about the valley in all directions. They were waving their trunks to and fro and squirming in their skins with laughter.

Bear decided that hide-and-seek with elephants was better fun than he had expected.   When they had stopped laughing and had gathered around, he said, ' Now it's our turn to hide.'   So off he went with Goat and Ostrich.

Monkey decided to stay behind with the elephants.   They put their ears over their eyes, and Monkey counted for them.

Bear and Goat each chose a clump of the tall grass and made their way into it.   But Ostrich found some sand a little way off and buried her head in it.   Bear plunged about in his clump of grass, and Goat plunged about in hers.   It was very stiff and strong and thick and much taller than they were.   In the distance they heard Monkey saying '. . . twenty-nine, thirty.'

When Bear got deeper into his clump of grass, he couldn't hear Monkey any more.   It was very dark.   He pushed his way around, but he didn't seem to be getting anywhere.   He waited for a while, but nothing happened and he couldn't hear anything.   The grass was so tall and thick, it seemed to stop any noise coming in from outside.

The same thing was happening to Goat in her clump of grass.   ' I don't expect they'll ever find me,' thought Goat; and waited.

After a while, Bear decided he didn't want to

stay in the long grass any more. So he lifted up his voice and shouted ' Ha! Ha! '

His voice seemed to die away amongst the grass; and still nothing happened. Bear began to get frightened. He started walking. Then he started running. The grass was so tall and thick he couldn't see where he was going and didn't seem to be getting anywhere.

'Help! Help!' cried Bear.

' Here we are,' said a voice just behind him. A strong trunk was wound round his neck and a kind elephant led him out of the grass into the valley. Bear saw another elephant leading Goat out of another clump of grass nearby. Goat was looking very bewildered. Lower down the valley, Bear saw Ostrich where he had left her when he plunged into the clump of grass, with her head still buried in the same piece of sand.

The elephants were laughing heartily. ' Found you, Bear and Goat,' they said.

' But we still haven't found Ostrich,' shouted out one of the elephants.

' But there . . .' began Bear, pointing. He couldn't finish the sentence, because an elephant clapped its trunk over his mouth.

' Be quiet, silly,' whispered the elephant. ' It makes Ostrich happy to think we can't see her. Don't spoil her fun.'

' It's very dangerous,' said another, ' for a short animal to walk into a clump of Elephant Grass when he's alone.'

' If you're not tall enough you may wander round for days and days in circles without finding your way out,' said a third elephant.

' Monkey kept his eyes open,' said the aged elephant, ' and told us which clumps you and Goat had gone into. So we watched the top of the grass waving as you and Goat rushed around inside until we decided it was time to show you the way out.'

' It was a horrible experience,' said Goat. ' I

shall never go near a clump of Elephant Grass again.'

Bear was a bit angry; but suddenly the wind changed and started blowing up the valley. He smelt food. ' I am hungry,' he said.

' Of course you are,' said the aged elephant. ' I quite forgot what a long way you'd come. One of the elephants stayed behind when we came out to meet you. He's got a wonderful lot of berries and nuts and honey and is getting an enormous supper ready.'

' Come along,' said Bear, hungrily.

' Wait a moment,' said the aged elephant. ' We've got to find Ostrich first.'

So all the elephants trumpeted loudly, ' Ostrich, where are you? Supper's ready.'

Then Ostrich lifted her head out of the sand, blushing with pleasure and pride. The elephants linked trunks. And off they marched together down the valley towards their supper.

VII

On to the Marble Mountain

THEY stayed at Ponky Poo for ten whole days.
The elephants were so jolly and kind. They
were enormous eaters, so that there was always
wonderful food and more than enough for everybody. Bear never had to apologize for being
greedy. There were wonderful things to drink as
well. The elephants used to gather loads and
loads of berries and spread them out in a huge
heap on the ground. Then they would stamp
around and squeeze out the juice and store it in
great big jars. They even made a special drink
out of honey, and Bear vowed he'd never tasted
anything so gorgeous in all his life. He used to
go off for great long runs up and down the valley
on his roller skates so as to make himself as thirsty
as possible.

In the daytime they went for walks, and ran
races, and played games; and Bear, Goat and
Monkey practised climbing on the rocks. In the
evening after supper, they would light a fire and
the elephants would tell them stories. The ele-

phants had lived so long and had such wonderful memories that they could have gone on for ever; and Bear, Goat, Ostrich and Monkey were always sorry when it was time to go to bed. One night, Monkey got out his pack of cards and made the elephants rock with laughter at the funny tricks he played. Then Goat suggested they should play a game. She chose Pelmanism. This is a game where you put all the cards face downwards on the ground. Each animal in turn looks at two cards, and if he turns up a pair it counts as a trick, and he has another go. Bear, Goat and Ostrich had played it so often with Owl at Mappin Villa that they thought they must be the cleverest animals in the world at it. But the elephants won every time. ' It's easy for us, you see,' said the aged elephant. ' An elephant never forgets.'

Bear, Ostrich and Monkey could happily have stayed at Ponky Poo for weeks. Ostrich kept on hiding, and the elephants kept on pretending they couldn't find her. And they were always telling her how beautiful she was, until she thought they were the nicest creatures in the world. Bear was happy eating and drinking and listening to all the stories the elephants told. Monkey was up to his tricks all day long, and the elephants thought it was huge fun. But Goat was restless.

She had always been like that. Never content with what she was doing. Always wanting to get on with something else. Climbing the rocks up the side of the valley reminded her of her home on the Marble Mountain.

' We must say " good-bye ",' she said, ' and get on with our journey.'

Now it was all very well for Goat. It would be easy for a climber like her to get out of Ponky Poo; and easy for Monkey, too. Bear was a little clumsy; but he had done a lot of climbing when he was a baby bear on the Marble Mountain, and he would get out in the end in his own scrambling way. But what about Ostrich? How was she going to get out?

' That's the worst of a silly bird that can't fly,' grunted Bear.

At first they thought she might try running up the slippery slope. If she ran fast enough she might get to the top before she slid down to the bottom again. She tried once or twice with a terrific flapping of feathers; but it didn't work. Every step she ran up she slid two steps back. In the end they decided that Goat and Bear would have to take it in turns to carry her up.

So very early one morning they said good-bye

to their friends, the elephants. Then Goat and Monkey started prancing up the cliffs from rock to rock, while Bear slowly scrambled up with his bell in his hand, and the jig-saw puzzle tucked under his arm, and with Ostrich clinging to his back. Half-way up, Goat waited until Bear came up. Then she took Ostrich on her back and they made their way right up to the very top.

They lay down to rest for a while and ate some of the buns and berries and nuts the elephants had given them for the journey. Bear felt very thirsty. He drank some of the lovely honey drink the elephants had given him. It made him feel very jolly. Far away in the morning mist they could see the peak of the Marble Mountain. They looked down into the valley below them and waved good-bye to the elephants. Then they set off again on their journey.

Bear had taken off his roller skates to climb up out of Ponky Poo. But now he put them on again, and they all moved at a fine pace. It wasn't long before they crossed the river, and soon they were walking through some trees beyond. They found it rather difficult to see where they were going in the trees, but Owl had told them once that if you were lost the best thing to do was to follow your nose. They decided Ostrich's nose would be the easiest one to follow and so they got along famously.

Just as the trees were beginning to thin out, they heard a roaring noise in

the distance behind them. The noise came nearer and nearer very rapidly until it was right overhead.

There was no time to look for sand, so Ostrich buried her head in a pile of leaves. Monkey hid under a bush. Goat lowered her head and prepared to fight whatever this terrifying creature might be. Bear stood his ground. He looked up as the thing passed overhead. It was an enormous bird. It flew with a swish that made

Bear's hair stand on end, and went away over the treetops getting lower and lower.

The noise got less and less as the thing went away into the distance, and suddenly stopped.

' Come along,' said Bear, trying to sound much braver than he really felt. ' It's only a bird. Let's go and find out what it's like and where it lives.'

' Only a bird, indeed ! ' said Ostrich. 'No bird I know makes a horrible noise like that.'

' Come along,' said Bear again. He walked slowly forward; and Goat bravely followed him, with Monkey on her back. Ostrich followed, too. It was terrifying; but better than being left alone in the forest with that fearful creature about.

After a while they came to a huge clearing. They took great care to keep hidden behind the trees. But peering out, they saw a most astonishing sight. Across the clearing ran long, straight roads as far as their eyes could see. At different places along the sides of the clearing were a number of enormous birds sitting quite still with their wings glistening in the sunlight.

One of the birds was quite near them, and suddenly two men came out of the trees nearby and walked up to it. Before they knew what was

happening there was a
roaring noise. The men
climbed up and dis-
appeared into the bird's
side. The noise became
louder and louder, and
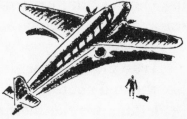
then the bird started running away from them
on wheels along one of the long, straight
roads.

' It uses roller skates, like me,' murmured Bear
excitedly.

As the bird got farther away it rose off the
ground and disappeared into the distant sky. It
was the most exciting thing they'd ever seen. In
the next hour two more birds flew away with men
inside them, and two other birds came down out
of the sky, ran along the roads on their roller
skates and came to rest by the side of the
clearing.

Monkey climbed to the top of one of the trees
to get a better view. Ostrich was thrilled by the
birds, but was frightened of the men and did her
best to hide. Bear and Goat wanted to know just
where they were. They did the jig-saw-puzzle
map Owl had made for them; and luckily the
piece they wanted wasn't missing. Sure enough,
just where they were standing on the map was a

big clearing, and written across it in large letters
was the word ' AERODROME '.

.⁑.

' Trust Owl to know all about a wonderful place
like this and not to tell us,' said Bear.

' I think it's the most exciting thing I've ever
seen,' said Goat. ' I should like to have a talk
with one of those wonderful birds.'

She crept away softly through the trees round
the edge of the clearing till she came to the place
where one of the birds was standing. She looked
cautiously around her to make sure that there
weren't any men about. ' Hi! ' whispered Goat.

The bird said nothing. ' Hi! ' said Goat more
loudly, and then ' Hi! ' louder still. The bird
went on saying nothing.

Goat crept out stealthily from the trees to have
a better look. It was a most peculiar bird. It
had what might be eyes in the front of its head;
and perhaps it used the blunt thing in front for a
nose. Goat couldn't see anything that looked
like a mouth, though she felt it ought to have an
enormous mouth to make such an enormous
noise. A door was open in the bird's side. Goat
peeped in and saw lots of snug and cosy seats. It
really looked a very comfortable bird for flying in.

Suddenly she heard voices. She hurried back

into the trees, hoping she hadn't been seen. Some men came up, stepped into the bird's side and shut the door. There was a roaring noise which got louder and louder, and then the bird flew away into the distance.

Goat joined the others and told them what she had seen. ' We shall have to remember this place,' she said; ' it might come in very useful one day. But now we must hurry if we're going to get to the Marble Mountain before the sun sets.'

So they made their way cautiously through the trees, keeping well away from the Aerodrome in case Man should see them. After a while they moved faster; and by the middle of the day they came out of the forest and found themselves on the edge of the Great Plain. In the distance ahead of them they could see the Marble Mountain.

They stopped to have something to eat. But they didn't waste much time. Even Bear was almost too excited to eat. Very soon they were on their way again. They crossed the Great Plain at a tremendous speed, going straight across the sands towards the Marble Mountain, with Ostrich running, and Bear on his roller skates, and Goat running with her head well down and Monkey perched on her back. Poor Goat couldn't keep up with the others, though she ran very fast. But when Bear and Ostrich got to the other side of the Great Plain they waited and collected some special berries to refresh her when she caught them up. Goat had forgotten quite how lovely the berries on the Marble Mountain could taste.

Then, all together, they started climbing up the Marble Mountain through the trees. The birds and the bees were thrilled to see Bear coming back to the Marble Mountain again. ' It's a surprise,' said Bear. ' Don't let my father and mother know I'm coming.'

So all the bees buzzed and the birds twittered, ' It's a surprise; it's a surprise.'

They passed through a clearing half-way up the mountain, and Bear stopped for a while to have some honey with the Queen Bee, who had been one of his best friends when he was a baby on the Marble Mountain. He introduced her to Goat, Ostrich and Monkey. While they were there, Eagle flew down from the top of the mountain.

' It's a complete surprise,' he said. ' Your mother has no idea that you're coming. She's baking an enormous cake in the mouth of the cave, and your father's lying down having a sleep.'

' Come on,' said Bear, eagerly. He thanked the

Queen Bee and promised to come and see her again. And then they set off again up the mountain.

' It's a surprise; it's a surprise,' the birds were twittering all around them.

On they went until the trees came to an end and ahead of them was the bare mountain. There, higher up the slope, was the cave where Bear had been born. There was his mother baking a simply tremendous cake. Bear's mouth watered. Of all the wonderful things they had had to eat at Mappin Villa, there was nothing so gorgeous and so satisfying as the cakes his mother used to bake.

' Hush! ' said Bear. All was quiet around the top of the Marble Mountain. Even the birds stopped twittering.

Then Bear lifted his enormous bell and holding it high in his two furry paws he swung it wildly to and fro. The noise echoed round the mountain-top.

Bear's mother heard the bell, just as she used to when he was a baby and rang it because he was lost on the mountain. Bear's father woke up and heard it, too. And they both came running happily down the mountain-side towards the trees—towards the sound of Bear and his bell.

Soon Bear was in his mother's arms, and she was

covering him all over with kisses. She led him and his friends back up the hill to the cave. It was warm and cosy inside.

It wasn't long before Goat slipped away; and soon a sound of happy bleating in the distance showed that she had joined her mother and father and all her uncles and aunts and brothers and sisters and cousins again.

But Bear sat on in the cave with his father and mother, hearing their news and telling them all about the happy time he had had in the forest. It was lovely to be home again. And his father and mother thought Ostrich was the nicest bird they had ever met and that Monkey was the jolliest of animals, apart of course from their own very special Bear.

It was long after sunset when Bear went to bed that night. There was so much to tell! He was very comfortable and happy, and when at last he went to sleep he dreamt the loveliest of dreams.

VIII

Fun on the Marble Mountain; Owl is sent for and makes a Plan

THE next few weeks were real summer weather. Bear was as happy as could be. His mother looked after him as only mothers can. There was always plenty to eat, and lots of friends coming in for parties.

Bear had forgotten quite how warm and comfy the cave could be. Of course, there weren't any beds to sleep in or shiny brass taps with ' HOT ' and ' COLD ' on them as there were in Mappin Villa. But Bear slept warm and snug, and his mother kept him clean by licking him all over, as she used to do when he was a baby. How proud she was to see what a fine, strong Bear he had grown into! He was as strong as his father, and used to go into the forest with him every day to pull up trees to make fires for the winter. Monkey helped him, with some of the branches from the trees, to build a fence round the mouth of the cave. He put a gate in the fence and on it he wrote ' BEARS' DEN '.

Bear had forgotten just how sweet the honey could taste when the bees came in off the heather. He had forgotten what fun it was to go exploring up the mountain-side, climbing from one crag to another and seeing the whole world spread out below him. He went to call on Goat, and one very clear day, when they were standing near Eagle's nest at the very top of the mountain, they saw the forest far away in the distance across the Great Plain; and they saw two wisps of smoke rising into the sky and knew that they came from the chimneys of Mappin Villa and Crosspatch Cottage.

'I wonder what Owl is having for breakfast,' said Bear.

Monkey soon made friends with everybody. But Ostrich began to feel very lonely. 'It was nice in the forest,' she said, 'because I was the only ostrich and you were the only bear, and Goat was the only goat. But now you and Goat are all jolly together with your families, and I feel lonely without any ostriches to run races with. Your mother is very kind to me; but sometimes I feel sad and want to go away and hide. And there isn't any sand up here on the mountain.'

'Why don't you go and find some other ostriches?' asked Bear.

' I don't know where to look for them,' said Ostrich. ' I've often told you how the wicked men took my mother away and put her in the Zoo. When I found she had gone, I ran after her for a long, long time, not knowing where I was going. I could never find my way back now.'

' Couldn't you ask some bird? ' asked Bear. ' They fly about all over the place and must know where the ostriches live.'

Ostrich gave him an angry look and walked away without saying a word.

' Now you've upset her, you silly,' said Goat. ' You know how sensitive she is about not being able to fly like other birds. Fancy telling her to ask a bird where the ostriches live. Now if you told her to ask an animal it would be different.'

' But an animal wouldn't know,' said Bear.

' Silly. He could ask a bird without letting Ostrich know,' said Goat. ' And then he could tell her as if he'd known himself all along.'

The more Bear thought about this idea, the cleverer it seemed. So he went to see Eagle early the next morning to ask him where the ostriches lived.

' It's easy,' said Eagle. ' They live two or three miles away towards the sunset. You could start after breakfast and be back in time for lunch.'

So Bear went back to the cave. And after breakfast he asked Ostrich to come for a walk with him. ' I've met an animal who knows where the ostriches live,' he said.

' An animal, did you say ? ' asked Ostrich anxiously.

' Yes.   An animal,' said Bear, firmly.

So they set off together, the way Eagle had said.

It was quite a long way; but Bear had his roller skates, and it was all downhill and before long they came out of the trees on to a broad, sandy plain which was just full of ostriches.

' Hurray! Hurray ! ' shouted Bear with excitement; and at once all the ostriches —

there must have been at least a hundred of them
—buried their heads in the sand. ' Look,' cried
Bear. ' There are your ostriches for you! '

Ostrich gazed anxiously around her. ' I can't
see any,' she said.

' But look, silly,' said Bear; ' there they are.
Hundreds of them! '

' I can't see any,' repeated Ostrich. ' They
must be hiding from me.'

So Bear skated away across the plain until he
came to one of the ostriches. He pulled its head
out of the sand, and Ostrich came running up
excitedly to join them. Bear left them together.
He went back into the trees and stayed for a little
while in hiding, watching.

One by one, the ostriches lifted their heads out
of the sand and gazed nervously around them.
Ostrich herself was just mad with excitement as
she saw them. Then all the ostriches came together in a bunch and went racing round and
round the sandy plain, squawking with happiness
and the fun of running so fast.

' Now Ostrich is happy at last,' said Bear to
himself. And he made his way back to the cave
near the top of the Marble Mountain where his
mother had got a lovely hot dinner waiting for
him.

But Ostrich still wasn't happy.   One afternoon, many days later, she came back to the cave.   Bear was out playing games with Goat.   They were jumping from crag to crag and sliding down the smooth slopes of the mountain.   Bear's mother was all alone.

' Well, Ostrich,' she said.   ' It is nice to see you again.'

' I've come back,' said Ostrich, ' because I'm still lonely.   I've had a lovely time in the valley with all the other ostriches.   We've run the most splendid races and had lots of fun.   But they've all got mothers, and my mother is far away in the Zoo.'

' Poor, dear Ostrich,' said Bear's mother, kindly.

' Bear is so happy with you,' said Ostrich. ' And Goat is so happy with her mother.   Though personally,' added Ostrich, ' I find Goat's mother rather too jolly.   I prefer somebody gentle like you.'

' Poor Ostrich,' said Bear's mother again. ' Come into the cave and keep warm.   I've got some lovely things for tea, and I expect my young son will be back soon.   You must come and live with us.   I know I can make you happy.'

So Ostrich came into the cave and made herself at home.   Bear soon came back from his party with Goat and was very happy to see Ostrich again. But Ostrich was very tired and soon fell off to sleep. So Bear sat up late, and his mother told him how Ostrich had come back and why. ' I'll do my best to make her happy,' she said. ' But it's not going to be easy for me to pretend to be mother to a bird, however fond I am of her.'

' There's only one thing for it,' said Bear. ' We'll have to organize an expedition to rescue Ostrich's mother from the Zoo. Though I can't imagine how we're going to do it,' he added.

❧

Bear hardly got to sleep at all that night trying to work out plans to rescue Ostrich's mother. None of his plans seemed to be any good. So soon after breakfast he went over the mountain to have a talk with Goat.

' There's only one thing to do,' said Goat, at once. ' We'll have to send for Owl.'

' You clever Goat,' said Bear. ' Why didn't I think of it before ! '

' It's not me that's clever,' said Goat. ' It's Owl.'

So they sent a bird with a message to tell Owl to come at once; and that evening, just as the sun was setting, Owl came flying in through the mouth of the cave.

Everybody was very pleased to see him again. Bear didn't want Ostrich to get excited; so he took Owl outside the cave and a little way down the mountain-side. Owl perched on a rock and Bear sat on the ground beside the rock so that he could whisper straight into Owl's ear without being overheard. He told Owl all that had happened since they had left Mappin Villa; and finished, ' Now we must make a plan to rescue Ostrich's mother and we know you're the only creature that can make it.'

' Very well,' said Owl. ' I have heard all you have said and now I must think. And let every bird and beast on the mountain keep silent all through the night; because if any bear grunts in his sleep or if any nervous bird coughs, I might stop thinking and have to start all over again from the beginning.'

So Bear tiptoed away. And he sent the birds flying round to all the creatures that lived on the mountain to tell them to keep silent all through the night; because Owl was thinking and it was most important that nothing should disturb him.

Then Owl flew up to Eagle's nest and asked if he could spend the night there alone; because the higher he was, the better he thought; and Eagle's nest was almost the highest place in the world.

Eagle was very glad to help and flew away to spend the night with a friend lower down the mountain, leaving Owl all alone.

Bear didn't dare to go to sleep in case he snored. He had never known the mountain so still and silent. Now and again he heard Owl calling, ' Tu whu; tu whit tu whu,' and knew he was getting an idea.

Then, an hour or two before the sun rose, a terrible noise shattered the silence. It was the great, deep buzzing roar of one of the monster birds they had seen on the Aerodrome on their way from Ponky Poo. ' Oh, dear! Oh, dear! ' thought Bear. ' Now Owl will forget everything and have to start all over again from the beginning.'

But when the noise died away into the distance, Bear heard Owl calling out, ' Tu whu; tu whit, tu whit, tu whit, tu whoo-oo-oo,' in tones of triumph.

' I believe he really has got an idea,' said Bear to himself. He turned over on his side and at last went off to sleep.

❧

Sure enough, Owl flew in the next morning as they were sitting outside the cave eating breakfast and watching the sun rise.

He perched on the gate that Bear had built.

He looked tired but happy. ' I've got a plan,' he said contentedly.

The others gathered round him eagerly, and Bear quickly broke the secret to Ostrich that they were making a plan to rescue her mother from the Zoo. They had never seen Ostrich cry before. She cried from sheer happiness and excitement.

' We shall want someone who is brave and strong,' said Owl.

' That will be Bear,' said Ostrich; and Bear blushed.

' We shall want someone who is very determined,' said Owl.

' That will be Goat,' said Ostrich.

' We shall want someone who is swift,' said Owl.

' That will be me,' said Ostrich.

' Or me,' said Bear, thinking of his roller skates.

' We shall want someone who is small and cheeky,' said Owl.

Monkey turned three somersaults in the air, landed on his feet and bowed.

' We shall want somebody who can talk like Man,' said Owl.

They thought about that one for a long time. They all tried to make noises like Man. ' Jabber, jabber,' said Monkey. ' Grunt, grunt,' said Bear.

' I know,' said Ostrich; ' we shall have to take Parrot with us.   Good old Parrot! '

' We shall want somebody who knows the way,' said Owl.

' That will be Swallow,' said Ostrich.   ' She goes to the Zoo every year and takes messages to my mother.'

' The trouble about Swallow,' said Bear, ' is that you can never get her to yourself.   She always flies around with hundreds of other swallows.'

' We shall insist on her coming alone,' said Owl.

' And lastly,' said Owl, ' we shall want someone who is very wise and clever.'

' Are you coming with us, Owl? ' asked Bear.

Owl nodded.

' Well,' said Bear, ' you're the wisest and cleverest creature I know.   If you come with us everything's bound to turn out all right.'

Then they all started asking questions until Owl hooted for silence.   ' Get all the others together,' he said, ' including Parrot;   and meet me by the edge of the Aerodrome at sunset to-night.   Now I must go away and get some sleep.   Please see that I am not disturbed.'

He flew away back to Eagle's nest, folded his wings over his chest, and went to sleep.

' What a remarkable bird,' said Bear's mother.
' Is he always like that ? '

' Nearly always,' answered Bear.   ' But I don't
know what we should do without him.'

He hurried off to tell Goat the news and to send
a message to Parrot to come and meet them that
evening at the edge of the Aerodrome.

Everybody on the mountain was thrilled and
longing for the day to come to an end.   But nobody dared wake Owl to ask him to tell them
some more about his plan.

IX

They fly across the Sea in a Great Bird

EVERYBODY has to keep quiet when an owl is thinking. That is why owls like to keep awake all night when everyone else is asleep. But owls think of wonderful things. So as the sun began to set behind the Marble Mountain, hundreds of birds and animals flew and crept very silently from all parts of the mountain and the forest towards the field where the great birds lived—'The Aerodrome', as Owl called it.

Everybody knew that something was going to happen; and no one wanted to miss the fun. ' Hush! ' said everybody to everybody else.

The sun set. The glow-worms and the fireflies shone in the darkness, but it was very cold. Bear, Goat and Ostrich jumped up and down to keep themselves warm. The swallows flew around high above the treetops. Monkey sat up in a tree whispering to Parrot. There were some lovely coco-nuts in the tree. He longed to pick them and drop them on the animals gathered below; but he didn't dare in case Owl should catch him at it and be cross.

They all got very anxious waiting for Owl. Would he never come? Bear teased Ostrich as he always did. He tweaked her feathers and asked her to fly up to Eagle's nest to tell Owl they were waiting for him. Monkey asked Parrot to fly and fetch him; but Parrot was very proud. ' I'm not used to being kept waiting,' he said. ' If that rude Owl doesn't come soon, I shall go home.'

There was a story that Owl had once gone to sleep for two hundred and fifty whole hours on end. Bear was afraid it might happen again. ' He looked very tired when I last saw him,' he whispered. ' It's all that thinking he does. It's much better to be fat and happy like me and never to think at all.'

In the distance a clock said ' Ding-dong, ding-dong'; and almost immediately afterwards a voice said ' Tu whu; tu whit tu whu '.

It was Owl. The animals gathered round him and listened eagerly as he explained his plan.

' We shall all of us have to be very calm,' said Owl. ' You see that great bird near us on the edge of the field.'

They all turned their heads round and looked.

' Well,' said Owl, ' I have heard that when the clock says " ding-dong " eight times and then strikes eleven, a man will step into the great bird and fly away. My plan is very simple. We shall go with him.'

Ostrich shuddered. She was terrified of Man. ' I'm sure he will take us to the Zoo,' she said.

' That, silly,' said Owl, ' is just what we want him to do. And when we get to the Zoo we shall rescue your mother and bring her home again.'

All the birds and animals started to cheer, but Owl silenced them with a violent ' Sh-h-h-h . . .'

' When the man comes up to the great bird he will open the door,' went on Owl. ' We must set a trap for him. Parrot will hide in a tree nearby and will call out to the man to lure him away.

Then we must run forward and creep into the great bird and hide. After that we shall see what happens. And everybody must be very, very quiet.'

' What is the man called? ' asked Parrot.

' I don't know,' said Owl. ' But most men are called " Bill "; and I expect that will do if you want to call him something.'

' And how do you think I shall get into the great bird myself? ' asked Parrot.

Owl couldn't think of an answer. ' Clever birds don't ask silly questions,' he said. ' Now keep quiet all of you. I want to think.'

Parrot flew off and perched on a great dark tree forty yards away from the great bird. Bear, Goat and Ostrich gathered on the edge of the trees as near to the great bird as possible. Monkey and Owl and Swallow sat up in the trees, waiting. Owl sent the glow-worms and fire-flies away so that nobody should be seen in the darkness. He made the other animals stand back so that they wouldn't be seen or get in the way. Hippopotamus coughed. He had been drinking too much muddy river water, and it always made him cough. It was a horrible noise. Owl sent him straight back home.

The time passed quickly. The clock in the distance said ' Ding-dong ' eight times and then started saying ' Boom '. As it said ' Boom ' for the eleventh time, a man came across the field in the darkness and walked up to the great bird. He opened a door. There was a click and lights went on inside, shining through a row of little windows. They could see the long body and the great wings stretched out. All the birds and animals held their breath until they thought they would burst. Elephant was holding so much breath, he felt as though he was swelling up like a balloon.

Suddenly a voice spoke in the darkness. ' Come over here, Bill,' it said ; ' come over here.'

The man turned round just as he was climbing into the side of the great bird. The voice spoke again. ' Come over here, Bill,' it said.

The man turned away from the great bird and walked across to see who was calling him.

' Now,' whispered Owl. He and Swallow flew towards the great bird, and Bear, Goat, Ostrich and Monkey crept out from behind the trees. Behind them they heard a hissing noise. Elephant couldn't hold his breath any longer. Luckily the man didn't hear ; or perhaps he thought it was the wind in the trees.

They soon reached the great bird, and all of them bundled inside. There was a seat in the front and they crouched down behind it, hiding.

' Sh ! ' said Owl, as Ostrich's teeth chattered with fright.

' Stop tickling me with your beard,' muttered Bear to Goat.

' Sh ! ' said Owl again.

There was a flutter at the door, and Parrot flew in and joined them. ' Heave-ho, my hearties,' said Parrot.

' Sh ! ' said Owl, yet again.

They waited a little while longer. Then the man came back. He stepped into the great bird, shut the door and sat down on the seat behind which they were hiding. He pressed a button, and the great bird said ' Whirr-whirr ', very loudly.

Ostrich longed for some sand to bury her head in.

The great bird said ' Whirr-whirr ' more loudly still and began to move forward, going bumpety-bump over the field. It went faster and faster, and then faster still. Suddenly it stopped bumping. They were in the air. The great bird flew round in a curve, going higher and higher all the time, and they could see the trees

below them.
Soon they were
flying right over the
top of the Marble Moun-
tain, high above Eagle's nest.

It was too much for Ostrich. All her
life she had been waiting for this to happen.
Here she was, a bird, up in the air at last! She
stood up and flapped her wings in triumph. ' I'm
flying! ' she squawked. ' I'm flying! '·

The man looked round at her in horror. ' It's
a bird,' he gasped.

' Not really,' said Bear, getting up and bowing.
' It's only Ostrich.'

'Birds fly,' said Ostrich angrily, 'and I'm flying.'

' It's a Bear,' gasped the man.

' Let me introduce you,' said Parrot, perching
on his shoulder. ' This is a man,' he said to the
others. ' And these,' he said, ' are my friends
Bear, Goat, Owl, Ostrich, Swallow and Monkey.
In case you don't know, you're taking us for a
ride.'

The man gulped nervously. ' I shall fly straight
back to the field,' he said.

' If you try to do that, I shall peck your eyes
out,' said Parrot.

' And I shall butt you,' said Goat.

' And I shall tickle you,' said Ostrich.

' And I shall hug you,' said Bear.

' And I shall tease you,' said Monkey.

' I shall know if you try to fly the wrong way,' said Swallow.

' Fly straight to the Zoo,' ordered Owl; ' and let there be no monkey business.'

' You mean " man business ",' said Monkey indignantly.

' Isn't Man funny! ' said Ostrich, giggling. ' He talks just like Parrot.'

' I think he talks like Mr Murgatroyd,' said Goat.

Ostrich stretched her long neck forward, twisted it round and looked into the man's eyes. ' It *is* Mr Murgatroyd! ' she exclaimed. ' It's that horrid man who teases animals.'

Ostrich was right. It was Mr Murgatroyd. There he sat, with the same unkind face, wondering how he could tease them. They were his prisoners inside the great bird. But perhaps, they thought, he was their prisoner, and would have to do what they told him, whether he liked it or not. They clustered round him. Mr Murgatroyd glared at them. And they glared back. Bear could stare for twenty minutes without blinking. And Owl never blinked after sunset.

' This will teach him to tease animals,' growled Bear.

' Fly on, you brute,' commanded Owl.

The man went white with terror. ' I'll do everything you ask me to do,' he stuttered.

' Fly on,' they all cried out together. And he flew on.

As the sun rose, they flew out over the sea. They were flying over the sea all day. As darkness fell, they came over land and before long they  were flying over an enormous town with a great river winding through it and lights winking for miles and miles along the streets and in the windows of hundreds and thousands of little houses. They came lower and lower and at last landed with a bump in the middle of a great green park. They heard the sound of animals roaring and knew they were near the Zoo.

X

They rescue Ostrich's Mother and fly back to the Marble Mountain

SWALLOW knew just where they were. ' This is Regent's Park,' she said. ' And that is the Zoo on the other side of those railings.'

Owl called for silence. ' Goat will stay here,' he said, ' to look after the man and see he doesn't try to escape.'

Goat lowered her head. She looked very determined and her horns looked very hard and strong. Mr Murgatroyd decided it would be better to stay where he was.

' You, Parrot,' said Owl, ' will fly away along the path and hide in one of the trees. If anybody comes along you must talk to him and tell him to go away again. We don't want anybody to interfere.

' You, Ostrich, will stay here; and if there is any trouble you must run and fetch us back at once.

' Swallow will fly on ahead to tell Ostrich's mother we're coming; and then she must fly back to show us the way.

' Bear and Monkey will come with me. And when it's all over, I shall call out " Tu whit tu whu ", and everybody must come back here and we'll fly away.'

Everybody nodded to show they understood. Parrot and Swallow flew off in different directions. Ostrich and Goat mounted guard over Mr Murgatroyd. Bear, Owl and Monkey set off together and soon came to the strong, high railings round the Zoo. Owl flew over and Monkey climbed over. Bear took two of the railings in his great strong paws and pulled them apart. He walked through the gap. They were inside the Zoo.

Swallow soon flew back and joined them.

' She's ready,' said Swallow. ' I left her brushing her feathers, and she was very excited.'

' I hope she doesn't squawk like that silly daughter of hers and give the game away,' muttered Bear.

They made their way past a rocky hill. There were hordes of jabbering monkeys on it, and they called out to Monkey to come and join them; but he put his fingers to his lips and said ' P-sss-t! '

They passed another rocky place where two white bears were lying fast asleep. Bear had never seen white bears before. He wanted to stop and ask them where they came from and if they weren't cold with all that snowy white fur. But Owl hurried them on.

They passed a long, gloomy house, and there was a loud, deep roar as they went by. ' Lion and Tiger live in there,' explained Swallow.

They came round a corner, and there at last was the cage with Ostrich's mother inside. It was open at the top. ' If only the silly bird could fly! ' thought Bear.

Ostrich's mother was overjoyed to see them and started running round and round the cage with excitement. Monkey climbed in over the top and joined her. He was very clever with his fingers and quickly started picking away at the lock to

try and open the gate and let her out. But it was
a very strong lock. Owl was getting nervous.
Any moment somebody might come along and see
them, or somebody walking through the Park
might find the great bird.

Bear looked at the bars of the cage. It was
only an Ostrich's cage. Perhaps, he thought, the
bars weren't very strong. He gripped them with
his paws to try.

Suddenly in the distance they heard a voice.
It was Parrot.

' Go the other way,' he was saying; ' go the
other way.'

' Hurry! hurry!' cried Owl. ' Something
must be happening out in the Park.'

Bear didn't wait any longer. He pulled at the
bars with all his strength. They were very strong
bars. But he was a very strong bear. Slowly
the bars bent apart. He puffed and grunted and
then pulled again. The gap widened.

' I think I can squeeze through,' said Ostrich's
mother.

She tried. She got half-way through. Then,
alas, she stuck.

They heard Parrot in the distance calling out
again, ' Go the other way, please; go the other
way.'

Far in
the dis-
tance some-
body blew
a whistle.
'Hurry! hurry!'
cried Owl.

Bear didn't
hesitate. He
seized Ostrich's
mother and pulled.
She squawked with
pain. But he pulled
harder, and suddenly
she came out of the
cage through the gap in
the bars—so suddenly
that Bear fell over back-
wards on the path.

'Quick! Quick! Back as fast as you can,'
cried Owl. Bear picked himself up and they
started running, with Swallow showing them the
way. Ostrich's mother had been in the cage for
so long, she had almost forgotten how to run.

Almost as soon as they were out of sight, some
men came running round the corner, roused by the
sound of the whistle in the distance. They saw the

gap in the bars and the empty cage.　They blew
their whistles.　' Ostrich has escaped,' they cried.

Then other men started blowing whistles in
other parts of the Zoo and crying out, ' Ostrich
has escaped.　Ostrich has escaped.'　All the birds
and the animals in the Zoo woke up and started
roaring and howling and hooting at the same time.
Such a noise had never been heard before.

Back in the Park, Ostrich, Goat and Parrot had
been getting more and more anxious.　Parrot had
met two old ladies walking along the path and had
persuaded them to go the other way.　But after
that, there came a keeper, walking through the
Park on his way to the Zoo.　He was very suspi-
cious and had blown his whistle.　Mr Murgatroyd had shouted ' Help! ', and although Goat
had butted him really hard and Ostrich had
clapped one of her wings over his
mouth so that nobody should hear
his screams, it was too late.　The
keeper had heard him.　He blew
his whistle again.　Then lots of
whistles started blowing inside
the Zoo; and they heard people
shouting ' Ostrich has escaped;
Ostrich has escaped! '

Swallow flew up to tell them

that Ostrich's mother was on the way and to warn them to be ready to start at once; then she flew back to guide the rescue party.

Parrot flew around through the trees away from the great bird calling out ' This way!   This way! '

The men came climbing over the railings out of the Zoo, and some of them followed Parrot. But others came running towards the great bird, following the first keeper, who had heard Mr Murgatroyd shouting for help.

Then Ostrich did a very brave thing.   She left the great bird and ran across the Park to the place where all the men were shouting and all the whistles were blowing.   They saw her almost at once. ' There she is! ' they all shouted.

' Hee!   Hee!   Can't catch me,' she squawked back.

They ran at her, and she ran around them and then led them across the Park right away from the great bird.   She pretended to be lame so as to give them a hope of catching her.   Other men joined in as she hopped away, always keeping just ahead of them.   The other animals heard the shouting and the whistling fading away into the distance.

Meanwhile, Ostrich's mother with Bear and Owl and Monkey had come out of the Zoo into the Park. They made their way quickly across the grass to the great bird. Goat was there, standing guard over Mr Murgatroyd. Parrot soon joined them. Swallow was there. Everybody was there except brave Ostrich.

Owl stood on the nose of the great bird. ' Tu whit, tu whu,' he hooted, as loudly as he could.

Ostrich, running away in the distance, heard him faintly. She knew it was the signal for all of them to go back to the great bird. She hobbled on a little farther, so as to take the men as far away as possible. Then she turned round. She circled round them. Then she stopped hobbling and started to run as only

Ostrich could run. She vanished like the wind and left the men standing still and gasping with surprise. She was back at the great bird in no time. They all jumped in and Bear slammed the door.

' Fly! ' commanded Owl.

' I won't,' said Mr Murgatroyd.

' Fly! ' commanded Bear, gripping Mr Murgatroyd's shoulders.

' I won't,' said Mr Murgatroyd, stubbornly.

' Fly! ' they all cried, gathering round him angrily.

Mr Murgatroyd heard the whistles blowing and the sound of men shouting coming nearer and nearer. He was still sore where Goat had butted him and knew that Bear was getting ready to hug him, that Ostrich would tickle him and Monkey would tease him. He could almost feel Parrot getting ready to peck him. But help was coming. He shut his eyes. ' I won't fly,' he said.

Monkey climbed forward. ' Throw him out of the window,' he said. ' If he isn't going to fly, I shall.'

Bear pulled Mr Murgatroyd away by his collar, and Monkey sat in the empty seat. He was a clever monkey. He had watched how the man flew and knew just what to do. He pressed a button and the great bird said ' Whirr-whirr '. It went on saying ' Whirr-whirr ' louder and louder and then it began to move slowly forward just as the men came running up, shouting angrily and blowing their whistles. They were too late. The great bird moved faster and faster and soon they were up in the air again.

Monkey looked round. He saw that Mr Murgatroyd was still there. ' Why didn't you throw him out of the window? ' he asked.

' Well,' said Bear, ' Swallow tells me there's a large pond in the Zoo in which the crocodiles live. I think they would like to meet Mr Murgatroyd. If you wouldn't mind flying over the pond, perhaps I could drop him in.'

So they flew back over the Zoo and came down very low. They saw the men they had left behind, waving their arms and shaking their fists angrily. They came down lower still and circled round. Then Bear opened the door and threw Mr Murgatroyd out. He made a lovely splash as he fell into the pond; and soon after there were some more splashes as the crocodiles dived in off the banks.

' I don't expect we shall see him again,' said Bear, as they flew away towards the sea.

' I should like to think the crocodiles would eat

him up,' said Goat; 'but I'm afraid he'd taste too nasty even for a crocodile.'

' I wish we had thought of throwing him to the alligators,' said Monkey. ' They don't mind what they eat.'

Ostrich said nothing. She was far too happy. She sat with her mother at the back of the great bird, thinking how wonderful it was to be together again.

Ostrich's mother said nothing. She was too happy even to say ' thank you '. How kind and clever everybody was; and how wonderful it was to have such a brave daughter. And how thrilling it was to fly!

Goat was busy teaching Parrot to play noughts and crosses. Monkey was busy flying; and Bear went over to watch how he did it. He hoped Monkey would let him have a try. It looked very easy.

Swallow never said very much, except to other swallows. Now and again she perched on Monkey's shoulder to show him the way; but most of the time she sat back quietly, thinking how nice it was to fly without having to flap her wings.

All was quiet except for the steady ' Z-z-z-z-z-z ' of the great bird.

Owl decided somebody ought to write a poem. He settled down to think. Surely there must be some word to rhyme with ' Ostrich '. He went on thinking until day began to dawn. Daylight always made him feel sleepy. He started snoring.

When he woke it was dark. The great bird was coming down lower and lower. Bear tapped him on the shoulder. ' Wake up, sleepy,' said Bear. ' We're going to land. Swallow and Parrot have flown away already. We had to stop Ostrich and her mother trying to fly away as well.'

Sure enough, they were back over the great field. As Owl blinked and looked around him there was a bump, and the great bird ran smoothly across the field towards the forest at the edge. Bear opened the door, and they all jumped out. From the distance they heard some men running towards them.

' Thank you,' gasped Ostrich and her mother. They flapped their feathers and ran off together into the darkness. Bear and Goat didn't wait. Off they hurried through the trees towards the Marble Mountain to let their mothers know they were safely home again. Monkey scurried off and climbed up into the trees.

'School again to-morrow,' thought Owl. He took one last look at the great bird and flew away.

When the men ran up to the great bird there was nobody there.